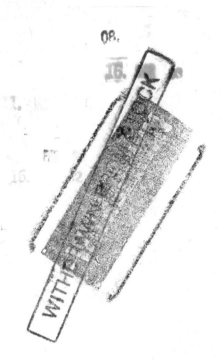

Nightlines

Nightlines

John McGahern

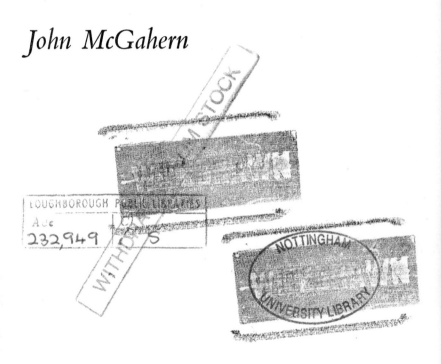

FABER AND FABER · London

First published in 1970
by Faber and Faber Limited
24 Russell Square London WC1
Printed in Great Britain by
Latimer Trend & Co Ltd Plymouth

ISBN 0 571 09257 8

1000356827

To

CHARLES MONTEITH

Contents

Wheels

Grey concrete and steel and glass in the slow raindrip of the morning station, three porters pushing an empty trolley up the platform to a stack of grey mail-bags, the loose wheels rattling, and nothing but wait and watch and listen, and I listened to the story they were telling.

"Seven-eights of his grave he'd dug in that place down the country when they went and transferred him up on promotion."

"Took to fishing out beyond Islandbridge, bicycle and ham sandwiches and a flask of tea, till he tried to hang himself from a branch out over the river but the branch went and broke and in he fell roaring for help."

"No use drowning naturally if you'd meant to hang yourself in the first place."

"Think there's any chance they'll have him up for attempted whateveritis?"

"Not nowadays—they'll give him a six-month rest-cure in the Gorman on full pay."

They'd filled the trolley, the smile dying in the eyes as they went past, the loose wheels rattling less under the load, the story too close to the likeness of my own life for comfort but it'd do to please Lightfoot in the pub when I got back.

"Looked at with the mind, life's a joke; and felt, it's a tragedy and we know cursed nothing," he'd said last night over the pints of Guinness.

Flush of tiredness in my face after the drinking, the jug of water by the bed had been no use, rough tongue, dry roof of the mouth, dull ache and throb of the poison along the forehead and on all the nerves, celebrating this excursion home, and always desire in the hot tiredness, the dull search about the platform for vacancy between well-fleshed thighs, may I in my relax-sirs slacks Hackney London plunge into your roomy ripeness and forget present difficulties.

The train drew in. I got a table in the restaurant car facing a priest and a man in his fifties, a weathered face under a hat, the blue Sunday suit limp and creased.

A black woollen scarf inside the priest's gaberdine almost completely concealed the Roman collar. The waiter brought us tea and toast on trays and the priest broke the silence.

"Have you come far?" he asked the hatted man at his side.

"From London, on the nightboat."

"You must work there then," the priest, in an interested politeness, continued.

"I do and fukken all, for the last twenty-eight years, on the buildings."

The man hadn't seen the collar and was unaware of the shock of the swear-word; the priest looked anxiously about the carriage but asked, "Is it tough on the buildings?" more to prove he could master the unsocial than out of any politeness now.

"Not if you use your fukken loaf like. You soon get wised-up that nobody'll thank you for making a fukken name for yourself by working. I'm a teaboy." The man was relaxed, ready to hold forth.

"And are you going home on holiday?" the priest changed.

"Not effin likely. I'm going home to bury the brother," he announced importantly.

"I'm sorry. May he rest in peace," the priest said.

"A release to himself and everybody else; been good for nothing for years."

The priest rose, he'd risked enough.

"If you're ever in London," the man held out his hand, "you'll find me any Sunday morning in the Archway Tavern, in the door of the Public Bar facing the Gents."

The priest thanked him, anxious to be gone, and as he turned to the door the man saw the round collar.

"That was a priest," he murmured as if waiting for the certainty to sink in. "Why didn't you tell me?"

"I got no chance."

"Well I'll be fukken blowed," he slumped.

"He didn't seem to mind too much. I wouldn't worry."

"Still he's a priest, isn't he, you have to draw the line fukken somewhere. I'll go and tell him I'm sorry."

"I wouldn't worry," I said, but he shambled to the door.

"He was all right about it, he said he understood," he informed when he returned after minutes, relief of confession on the old face as he pondered, "Tidy how a body can put his fukken foot in it."

The train had crossed the Shannon, the fields were slowing, I took the suitcase and shook hands with the man.

The front door was open when I came, and she was on her knees in the hall, scrubbing the brown flagstones.

She must have heard the iron gate under the yew at the road and the steps up the unweeded gravel but she did not stop or look up until I was feet away. All she said was my name, but all the tense emotion of the face, the tears just held back, went into the name, and it was an accusation. "Rose," I answered with her name.

I thought she was going to break, and there was the embarrassment of the waiting silence, the still brush in her hand beside her knees on the wet stone.

"Did you get the letter that I was coming?"

"Your father got a letter," her face hardened, and it was already a hard greying face, the skin stretched tight over the bones, under the grey hair.

"Was it all right to come then?"

She still didn't rise or make any sign for me to enter and when she dipped the brush in the water and started to scrub the stone again I put the suitcase down close to the wall of the house and said, "I'll fool around then till he comes," but she didn't answer and I could hear the rasp of the scrubbing brush on the stone till I'd gone the other side of the house.

They'd net-wired a corner of the orchard off for her hens, the wild nettles growing coarse and tall out of the bare scratched earth; henshit enriches the clay I'd heard them say.

"Be quiet, trembling between timidity and the edges of violence as the rest of your race, and wait for him to come, life has many hours, it'll end."

The bell without rope or tongue hung from the stone

archway where the pear-tree leaned; it used to call the workmen to their meals.

"Why don't you go to night lectures and try for promotion?" Lightfoot had asked, pints on the marble of the Stag's Head.

"I don't want."

"Wouldn't it be better for you to have some say than to have jumped-up jacks all the time ordering you around."

"Drink your drink. They have piped music in the office now. They talk less."

I saw my father come on the tractor, two creamery cans on the trailer, old felt hat on his head; I wondered if the sweat-band stank as it used or if it was rotten now. I watched him take the cans off the trailer, then go inside, body that had started my journey to nowhere.

The suitcase was still against the wall of the house. I left it there, but went in. One place was laid on the table by the window, and she was bent over saucepans.

"Your father has come from the creamery. He's gone out again but he'll soon be in for his dinner."

"Thanks. It's all right."

As I grow older I use hardly anything other than these formal nothings, a conciliating waiter bowing backwards out of the room.

I took the newspaper, went through the daily calamities that spice the well-being or lighten trouble with news of worse, in the gnawing silence the turning of the pages loud above the sounds of cooking. At last she took the whistle from the nail on the wall, blew three short blasts from the flower-garden.

Clay muffled his boots as he came in, leaving a trail on

the washed stone. I stood but he turned past me to the table as if he hadn't seen.

"Is the dinner ready, Rose?"

"In a second, Jim."

He drummed an idle rhythm with the bone of the knife on the cloth until she put the plate before him, fried eggs and bacon, a yellow well of butter in the middle of the creamed potatoes.

"There, Jim."

"Thanks, Rose."

The knife and fork rang often on the plate to break the aggressive sucking and swallowing of the food but he said nothing.

"I came on the train," I offered, and had to smile at how foolishly it hung in the silence till he took his hat with the flourish of a man-in-a-hurry, the sweat-band still apparently intact, and went in the direction of the timber-stack.

When he'd gone she put my plate on the table, "There's some dinner."

"Why didn't he speak? Does he not want me in the house?" I asked quietly as I ate.

She was stirring a mixture of meal and skim milk in a bucket for the calf with a stick.

"Do you know, Rose?" I'd to ask again.

"It's not my place to interfere, it'll only drag more trouble into it."

"Well I'll ask him myself then."

"What do you want to go and upset him for?" her voice was sharp.

"No, I can't stay here without knowing whether he wants me or not, the place is his."

"If you let it go today it'll calm down and tomorrow it'll be as if nothing had happened," she reasoned in her care but I could feel the hatred, the disappointment and pain had hardened with the years, but she could mask them better now.

In the confidence of her first days in the house she'd taken down the brown studio photo of the old wedding *Warner Artist Grafton Street*, replacing it with the confetti strewn black-and-white of her own, the sensible blue costume in place of the long white dress to silver shoes, she'd been too old for white.

Against her hopes, too old for children too, the small first communion and the confirmation photos stayed on the sideboard, replaced by no other, only disappearing when the youngest left and they were alone.

All remembered her near madness in the middle of her months as she felt the last years slip.

"Do I disgust you so much that you'll no longer touch me?" waking the sleeping house.

"For Chrisake don't you know there's children listening. I'm tired and shut up and let me get to sleep."

"You should have stuck with your children to the grave."

The noise of the blow came, and she escaping to the fields, losing herself between the tree trunks till she'd grown cold and came in to sit numbly in a chair over the raked fire till morning. Perhaps she'd hoped he'd come, but he hadn't, stiff with anger at the shouted insult to his maleness, more bitter since it echoed his own bitterness at growing old. The next day he'd dug the potatoes where the sheets hung on the line between two trees above the ridge,

B

scattering clay on the sheets she'd scrubbed white for hours on the wooden scrubbing-board.

It'd been years ago, and now they were alone, and he was her child and everything now. I could understand her care and hatred, whatever good that was since they seemed to come to the one thing, but it was getting late, and I didn't want to stay.

I found him splitting lengths of beech beside the useless pier he'd built to absorb the glass about the house, dangerous with jagged bits. He held the length steady with his boot against the pier while he drove the wedge into the timber. I waited until it split, and the wedge fell loose.

"Can I speak to you?"

As he turned to put another length of beech into position, I said, "If you don't answer I'll just leave."

"Well, I'm not in America as you can no doubt see," he suddenly turned.

"I can't understand why you've not spoken to me since I came."

"You're joking surely. Do you mean to tell me that you don't know why?"

"I don't know. I'd not ask you if I knew."

"You mean to say you know nothing about that letter you wrote in the spring?" he accused, the voice breaking under the whole day's resentment, starting to sob. "I had to wait till near the end of my days for a right kick in the teeth."

There was the treacherous drag to enter the emotion, and share and touch, the white lengths of beechwood about his boots and the veins swollen dark on the back of the old hands holding the sledge. With his sleeve he wiped away tears, as a child.

"The one important thing I ever asked you couldn't even be bothered," he accused.

"That's not true. When you wrote you wanted to move to Dublin I went round the auctioneers, sent you lists, looked at places."

"And you said if I did get a place and moved that you wanted no room in it."

"I want to live on my own, I didn't want you to come thinking differently."

"I didn't come under illusions. You took good care of that," he accused bitterly. "And I was foolish enough to think there might be more than pure selfishness."

I knew the wheel: fathers become children to their sons who repay the care they got when they were young, and on the edge of dying the fathers become young again, but the luck of a death and a second marriage had released me from the last breaking on this ritual wheel.

"You are married," I said, it was a washing of hands.

"Yes, I'm married," he said in a bitterness, close to regret. "What's that got to do with it?"

"What did she think of you leaving?"

"She'd be hardly likely to stay here on her own if I went," he resented the question.

"It's your life and her life, for me to enter it would be simple intrusion, and I don't want it, in the long run it'd cause trouble for everybody."

I could hear the measured falseness of my own voice, making respectable with the semblance of reason what I wanted anyhow.

"I'd give anything to get out of this dump," he changed.

"It's quiet and beautiful," the same hollowness came, I

was escaping, soothing the conscience as the music did the office.

"Quiet as a graveyard," he took up. "And stare at beauty every day and it'll turn sicker than stray vomit. The barracks shut now, a squad car in its place. Sometimes children come to the door with raffle tickets, that's all. But there's plenty of funerals, so busy Mrs. McGreevy's coffin last month came out roped on the roof of the bread van, and the way they talked about her was certain proof if proof was needed that nobody seriously believes in an after-life. They were sure they'd never hear the edge of her tongue again either in hell or heaven or the duck-arsed inbetween. I'd give anything to get out," he said with passion.

There was silence but it was easier after he'd spoken. Then he asked, "Are you down for long!"

"I'll stay till tomorrow if it's all right."

"That's about as long as you can stand us I suppose."

"It's not that. I have to be at work."

I helped him gather the tools.

"I think Rose is giving you your old room. I want to get the last things done before night."

"I've left your case in your old room, the bed is aired," she said when I came in.

"There's no trouble any more but I have to go tomorrow, it's to be back at the office," I explained.

"The next time you must come for longer," it was easy in the lies that give us room.

"I'll do that and thank you."

Quietly the dark came, the last tasks hurried, a shift of hens on the roost of the hen-house before the bolting of the door; and inside the lamp was lit and he said, "That's another day put down," as he took off his boots and socks, reek of feet and sweat as he draped socks over the boots on the floor.

"Rose, the corns were tormenting me no end today. Any chance you'd give them a scrape with the razor?"

"You better soak them first," she answered.

She placed a basin of steaming water by his chair on the floor, the water yellowing when she added Dettol. She moved the lamp closer.

He sat there, her huge old child, soaking his feet in water, protesting as a child. "It's scalding, Rose," and she laughing back, "Go on, don't be afraid." And when she knelt on the floor, her grey hair falling low, and dried the feet that dripped above the lighted water I was able to go out without being noticed as she opened the bright razor.

Cattle and a brown horse and sheep grazed on the side of the hill across the track, the sun came and went behind white cloud, and as it did the gravel shone white or dulled on the platform.

"The train won't go without you unless I tell it," the one official said to an anxious passenger pressing him to open the ticket office and went on stacking boxes on the gravel where the goods van would come in. When he did open the office and sold tickets there was still time left and the scrape of feet changing position on the gravel grew more frequent.

I had no hangover and no relax-sirs desire and as much reason to go back as come. I'd have hangover and desire in the morning and as much reason then as now. I was meeting Lightfoot in the bar beside the station and would answer "How did it go?" with how it went, repetition of a life in the shape of a story that had as much reason to go on as stop.

I walked through the open carriages. There was nobody I knew. Through the windows the fields of stone walls, blue roofs of Carrick, Shannon river. Sing for them once First Communion Day *O River Shannon flowing and a four-leaved shamrock growing* silver medal on the blue suit and white ankle socks in new shoes. The farther flows the river the muddier the water: the light was brighter on its upper reaches. Rustle of the boat through the bullrushes as we went to Moran's well for springwater in dry summers, cool of watercress and bitterness of the wild cherries shaken out of the white-thorn hedge, black bullrush seed floating in the gallons on the floorboards, all the vivid sections of the wheel we watched so slowly turn, impatient for the rich whole that never came but that all the preparations promised.

Why We're Here

Gillespie tested the secondhand McCullagh chainsaw as soon as he came from the auction, sawing some blown-down branches stacked against the wall of the house into lengths for firewood. The saw ran perfectly.

"Now to get rid of the evidence. For it'll not be long till he's up with his nose smelling unless I'm far out," he said to the sheepdog when he'd finished. He carried the saw and sawn lengths into the shed, scattering the white sawdust wide into the grass with his boot. Then he farted. "A great release that into the evening, thank God," he sighed, as he waited for the aroma of the decomposing porter he'd drunk in Henry's after the auction to lift to his nostrils, his eyes going over the ground beside the stack of blown-down branches again. "Not much evidence left that I can see. Nothing to do now but wait for him to arrive up."

He was waiting at the gate when Boles came on the road, the slow tapping of the cattle cane keeping time to the drag of the old feet in slippers, sharply calling HEEL to his dog as a car approached from Carrick, shine of ointment over the eczema on his face as he drew close.

"Taking a bit of a constitutional, Mr. Boles?"

"The usual forty steps before the night," Boles laughed. The two dogs had started to circle, nosing each other, disturbing the brown droppings of the yew. They stood in its shade, where it leaned above the gateway.

"Lepping out of your skin you are, Mr. Boles. No holding the young ones in these days."

"Can't put the clock back. The old works winding down, you know."

"No future in that way of thinking. You're good for ten Beechers yet, if you ask me."

They watched the dogs trying to mount each other, circling on the dead droppings of the yew, their flutes erect, the pink flesh unsheathed; and far off an ass braying filled the evening with a huge contentment.

"At much, this weather?" Boles asked.

"The usual foolin' around. Went to the auction."

"See anything there?"

"No, the usual junk, the Ferguson went for a hundred. Not fit to pull you out of bed."

"Secondhand stuff is not the thing, a risk, no guarantee," Boles said, and then changed to ask: "Did I hear an engine running up this way an hour ago?"

"None that I know of."

"I'd swear I heard an engine between the orchard and the house an hour ago."

"Country's full of engines these days, Mr. Boles. Can't believe your ears where they come from."

"Strange." Boles was dissatisfied, but he changed again to ask: "Any word of Sinclair this weather?"

"The crowd up for Croke Park saw him outside Amiens Street with an empty shopping bag. They said he looked shuck. Booked close enough to the jump."

"Never looked very healthy."

"*The ignorance and boredom of the people of this part of the country is appalling, simply appalling*," Boles mimicked an English accent quietly. "That's the speech he'll make to Peter at the gate. A strange person."

"Touched, that's all, I got to know his form well, the summer I bought this place from him and was waiting for him to shunt off. Especially when I was close to the house, mowing with the scythe there between the apple trees, he used to come out and spout to the end of the world. The ignorance and the boredom but nothing about his own, bad manners and the rain, speaking as one intelligent man if you don't mind to another, O Saecula Saeculorum world without end Amen the lord deliver us. He even tried to show me how to put an edge on the scythe."

"I knew him fifteen years here."

"Fifteen too long, I'd say."

"No, he was a strange person. He suffered from the melancholy."

"But he had a pension, hadn't he, from that cable in Valencia?"

"No, it wasn't money troubled him."

"*No reason why we exist, Mr. Boles. Why we were born. What do we know? Nothing, Mr. Boles. Simply nothing. Scratching our arses, refining our ignorance. Try to see some make or shape on the nothing we know*," Boles mimicked again.

"That was his style, no mistaking, nature of the beast. The way he used treat to that wife of his was nobody's business."

"In Valencia he met her, a girl in the post-office. He used to cut firewood in the plantation, I remember, and he'd blow a whistle he had when he'd enough cut. She'd come running with a rope the minute she'd heard the whistle. It was a fair sight to see her come staggering up the meadow with a backload of timber, and him strolling behind, golfin' at the daisies with the saw, shouting *fore*."

"Poor soft bitch. I knew a few'd give him fore, and the size of him in those plus fours. He should have stayed where he belonged."

"*I am reduced to the final ambition of wanting to go back to look on the green of the billiard table in the Prince of Wales on Edward Road. They may have taken it away though. Sign of a misspent youth, proficiency at billiards,*" Boles mimicked again.

"On the same tack to me in the orchard. A strange coot. Luther's idea about women. The bed and the sink. *As good to engage a pig in serious conversation as a woman. All candles were made to burn before the high altar of their cunts.* I'll not forget in a hurry how he came out with that spiff."

"He had a curious blend of language sometimes," Boles said.

"And he ends up after all his guff with an empty shopping bag outside Amiens Street Station."

"A lesson, but I liked him. Great smell of apples in the evening."

"Rotting on the ground. Wouldn't pay you to gather. Except a few hundredweight for Breffni Blossom. They don't mind the bruises."

"Better than wastin' in the grass."

The passing cars had their headlamps on now. A mile away, over fields of stone walks, the lighted windows of the 9.20 diesel rattled past.

"Train to Sligo."

"Empty, I suppose."

"I suppose. . . . Time to be moving in the general direction of the bed."

"No hurry, long enough lying down in the finish. How is the eczema?"

"Stays quiet long as I don't go near timber. I've got this stuff on to keep the midges off," he brushed his finger lightly along his cheek.

"If everything was right we'd appreciate nothing."

"Still, I'd have sworn I heard a chainsaw up this way today," Boles said as he turned to the road.

"Must have been from elsewhere," Gillespie contradicted. "What the wind can do with sounds is no joke."

"There was hardly a puff of wind today."

"Surprising what even a little can do, as the woman said when she pissed in the sea." Gillespie laughed aggressively.

"I was certain, but time to go," Boles said and called his dog.

"No use detaining you if you have, though it's young, the night, yet."

"Good night then."

"'Night, Mr. Boles."

He watched him go, the light tapping of the cattle cane in time to the drag of feet in slippers, calling HEEL to the dog as headlamps flooded the road from Boyle.

"That's what'll give him something to think about," Gillespie muttered as he called his own dog back and turned towards the house.

Coming into his Kingdom

"They're in love, they're in love, they're in love! Nora's in love with Stevie," the crowd of children cried at the fallen girl and boy.

They'd been struggling to sit in the Chair, a little hollow in the roadside ditch, on their way home from school. In one of the struggles Stevie had managed to get hold of the Chair, but before he could grip the grass or dig his heels into the clay Nora had jerked him out with all her weight. And when he came so easily with her she overbalanced on to the road, her grip tightening desperately on his arm to drag him down on top of her. His forehead struck heavily against her jaw, and they lay stunned together on the road for a moment, his mouth on the flesh of her side-face between the ear and outer roots of the hair, his body solidly on hers, his legs thrown between her opened thighs.

There was an anxious silence, fear of the injury that'd ruin their game, till someone shouted, "They're in love." The cry went through the crowd, raggedly taken up at first, though soon it grew to almost a chant.

"They're in love! They're in love! They're in love! Nora's in love with Stevie!"

Nora, a blonde girl of thirteen, quickly woke to what the shouting was about and pushed the stunned boy loose with her palms: his knee caught her dress as he rolled and bared the white young flesh of her thighs from the brown as far as the knees to the legs of a faded blue knickers.

"Nora has blue drawers," the jeer changed as the girl rose to her feet, instinctively smoothing her dress down, taut with shame and anger that broke in violent sobbing. She lifted her school-bag, burst through the circle of children, and began to run. They chased her down the earthen road between the sloe bushes to call, "Nora's mad in love! Nora has blue drawers! Nora's goin' to marry Stevie," but when someone shouted, "Nora's goin' to have a baby," it stopped as suddenly as it began. They'd gone too far. They slowed. Nora went out of sight at the next turn of the road. The stragglers and Stevie caught up with the main group. They looked about the fields and road, afraid they'd been observed. The whole thing could easily lead to trouble. They began to go quickly home, little conversation now, the group thinning as children said good-bye to each other till the next day and turned up the lanes to their farmhouses. After a mile only Stevie and a girl as old as Nora were left. They had to walk another whole mile of road to the village, climb Cox's Hill on the way.

Their canvas shoes dragged rustling through the dead leaves as they walked, in the frozen loneliness of the country in October, men digging potatoes alone in fields of long ridges where only the weeds were green, the sea of stalks on which blossoms rode in June dead and grey as matchwood. Neither of them spoke as they climbed Cox's Hill, their eyes bent on the drag-drag of their canvas shoes uphill through the leaves, the noise of someone shouting angrily at a horse beginning to drift from the woods across the river. There was only this silence between them, and he had longed for the moment they'd be alone as now, hurt and shamed by the shouting that he couldn't understand. He was waiting for her to speak but the only sound that came was the rustling of her canvas shoes uphill through the leaves.

"They cheered and shouted," he had to fumble at last. "They cheered and shouted when I fell on Nora."

The girl's eyes stayed on the leaves that she was now kicking uphill as she walked.

"They cheered and shouted," he was growing desperate. "Teresa, they cheered and shouted when I fell on Nora." This time she did look up and stared so coldly at him that he flinched: the terrible stare without compassion of the strong, it knows it can give life or grind it underfoot; but the other life is not what it needs, so it will pass on, impatiently shaking off its clinging burden; and if it does pause, it's but to amuse itself a while.

"They cheered and shouted," she admitted.

"But why? I only fell on Nora."

"What does it matter why? They cheered and shouted, that's all."

"But there must have been some reason?"

"You fell on Nora."

"But why did they shout?"

"That's the why," she laughed.

"But that's the why is no answer. Was there some reason for it?"

"There's a reason for everything."

"But why, Teresa? Why did they shout?"

"Why should I tell you?"

"No why. Just tell me."

"You're too young. You'll have to wait to find out. Why should I be the one to tell you? Answer me that and I'll tell you."

"You're not that much older than me," he argued painfully and doggedly and without much hope.

They'd reached the top of the hill. Before them, against the lake with its swaying barrels and Oakport Wood turning to rust beyond, great beech trees, was the village where they lived; the scattered shops and houses and humble sycamores of the roads dwarfed by the church in its graveyard of old yew and cypress trees. Past it the Shannon flowed, under the stone bridge at its end, flinting river of metal moving endlessly out into the wastes of pale sedge that waited for its flood waters to rise.

"I don't see what harm it would do you to tell," he pleaded.

"You'll have to grow up," she laughed the animal laugh of her superiority. Soon she'd be a woman in her prime, already her body was changing. She laughed again without turning her head and started to run downhill. He moved to keep with her, but he was too sick at heart, he let her run. He felt the same futility and confusion of everything as when his mother had gone away for ever, the terror and pain of his whole life draining away. Then something frighteningly alluring in the running girl's stride stirred him to follow her, but he was again bewildered by the memory of the softness of Nora's body, the shame of the shouting ringing in his ears. "They're in love! They're in love! They're in love!" and he began to weep with anguish.

The schoolroom was tense all through the next morning. They waited for what Master Kelly would say after prayers and it was with such relief they heard him say what he said every morning, "Open your home exercises and come up in your proper order, the fourth class first, and leave them on the table." They watched the road and concrete steps down to the school for someone to come and complain, and no one came. Every move of Nora's was watched, every move of Stevie's, every hand that went up to ask to go to the lavatory. The growing tension followed them to the playground, the boys in one group, the girls apart in another, Nora strung tight and eating her lunch alone by the wall. Then suddenly, and unnaturally as if she was the mouthpiece of a decision, one of the older girls called a game, and declared, "Nora must be Queen. Come on, Nora, we're making you the Queen," and they'd gathered round her and soon the air was filled with the excited noises of their play and the boys started to kick an old rag ball made from corks and the wool of ripped socks about at the other end of the yard. Stevie watched the tenseness go in the play, connected in some way to the fit of shrieking at the Chair the evening before. "They're in love! They're in love! They're in love!" still haunting him with his own helplessness and failure, but he'd try once more to get behind the mystery of it all. He would offer Teresa a penny toffee bar to tell on their way home.

Quickly they chased past the Chair that evening, they didn't even think of stopping. "It was nearly winter, the summer had gone, the ground was gettin' too damp for playin' on," and in ones and twos and threes they branched up their laneways till the girl and boy were left alone on the road to the village again. No rain had fallen, and their canvas shoes dragged rustling through the dead leaves as they set to climb Cox's Hill as on every other school evening of their lives.

"Why were they all so quiet today? Was it because of the Chair, Teresa?" he at last began.

She didn't answer for a long time: and then she smiled, inwardly, sure of her superiority, "It might be."

"But why, why did they cheer?" Her playful nonchalance was enough to rouse his anxiety to desperation.

"You don't know very much, do you?" she said.

"No, but can't you tell?"

"You don't know how you come into the world, do you?" she said, and he was shocked numb. He'd been told so many ways. He couldn't risk making a greater fool of himself before Teresa. There was so much confusion.

"No," he admitted. "Do you know?"

"Of course I know. Mammy explained everything to me and Maura ages ago, a day we were over at the bathing place in the lake. When we were drying ourselves with the towels after swimmin' she told us everything."

He'd grown hot and excited, whether it was from his desperation to know or the picture of lake and bathing suits and the woman talking mysteriously to the girls while they dried their naked bodies with the towels: but he was shocked cold again when she added, "That's the cause they shouted when you fell on Nora."

They shouted "You're in love" when he fell on Nora, he grasped back, desperate. What had the fall on Nora got to do with the way he'd been born? If they were the same thing, all Teresa had to do was to tell, a few words, and

c

everything'd be explained. The cries at the Chair, the fear all day would be explained—everything would. There'd be no more suffering.

If he'd been quiet and had pretended not to care very much she'd probably have told him then, but immediately he produced the toffee bar, she stiffened.

"If you tell me, I'll give you the bar," he told her softly.

"Tell you what?"

"How we be born, why they shouted," he had to say.

"Why should I tell you? Tell you for a toffee bar and commit a mortal sin by telling you?" and she was striding quickly ahead.

"It can't be that much harm to tell and the toffee bar is new, I got it in Henry's yesterday," he pleaded, the knowledge so awful now with the dark halo of sin about it that he despaired of its ever being given to him.

"Have you anything else to give? A toffee bar isn't enough?" she began to relent and his heart beat. Her eyes were greedy on the bar in his hand, tiny scarlet crowns on its wrapping. He had one thing more, the wheel of a clock, the colour of gold, and it could spin.

"There's nothing else," he warned anxiously.

"Give them to me first."

"And then you won't tell?"

"I'll cross my heart."

She thumbed the rough shape of a cross on her dress and he gave her the bar and wheel.

"Now," he urged when she seemed reluctant to begin.

"I don't know how to start," she said.

"You crossed your heart."

"You have to try and guess first."

"You crossed your heart to tell."

"Can you not think?" she ignored. "Do you not remember as we came to school Monday? Moran's bull and
Guinea Ryan with the cow? Can you not think?" she
urged impatiently.

The black bull in the field last Monday as they came to
school, the chain hooked to his nose, dragging Moran towards the cow that Guinea held on a rope halter close to the
gate. The cow buckling to her knees under the first savage
rise of the bull. He shuddered at what he'd watched a
hundred times related to himself: all the nights his father
had slept with his mother and done that to her; he'd been
got that way between their sheets; he'd come into the
world the way the calf came.

"Can you not think?" the girl was urging.

"Is it like the bull and the cow?" he ventured. It couldn't
be, it would be too fantastic, and he waited for her to
laugh.

Instead, she nodded her head vigorously: he had struck
on how it was.

"Now you've been told," she said. "That was why they
cheered when you fell on Nora."

Suddenly it was so simple and so sordid and so all about
him that it seemed he should have discovered it years before.

They were silent now as they went downhill home, a
delicate bloom on the clusters of blue sloes along the road,
the sudden gleam of the chestnut, or the woollen whiteness
of the inside of a burst pod in the dead leaves their shoes
went rustling through. "They're in love! They're in love!"
coming again to his ears but it was growing so clear and
squalid that there was hardly anything to see.

The whole world was changed, a covering torn away; he'd never be able to see anything the same again. His father had slept with his mother and done that to her, the same father that slept with him now in the big bed with the broken brass bells and rubbed his belly at night, saying, "That's what's good for you, Stevie. Isn't that what you like, Stevie?" ever since it happened the first night, the first night he'd explained in the slow labouring voice how the rubbing eased wind and relaxed you and let you sleep.

He'd come out of his mother's body the way the calf came—all at school had seen the calves born on their farms. And in Aughoo churchyard, at the back of the sacristy and under the shade of the boundary ash tree, his mother's body was now buried; the body his father had done that to, out of which he'd come; the body in a rotting coffin, under the clay, under the covering gravel. N.T. was after her name on the limestone cross they'd bought in Smith's for £30. They'd lifted three withered daffodils out of the jam jar when they'd visited it last July, weeded the daisies and dandelions out of the white gravel. And there had been viciousness too over the shrub of boxwood their aunt had planted on the grave, it had already taken root, and their father had torn it up in anger. He'd called to their aunt's house on their way home, shouting that she had no business interfering with his wife's grave and he didn't want to have them rooting up a stupid tree when it came to his own turn to go the way of all flesh.

The boy sobbed as his feet went through the leaves. He had been shattered by his mother's going, the unexpected mention of her name could still break him, but even that was growing different. His mother had lain down naked under his naked father years ago, his beginning. Though it was good to stand in the daylight of the others for once and not to be for ever a child in the dark.

As he walked his wondering changed to what it would be like to rise on a girl or woman as the bull rose, if he could know that everything would be known. If he could get Teresa to lie down for him some evening on their way, behind the covering of some sloe bushes—could he ever bring himself to ask her to do that for him? His body was tingling and hot as the night in convalescence he'd watched his mother undress and get into the bed that she'd moved into his room at the height of his illness, snowflakes drifting round the windows that winter evening and robins about the sills, the room warm and bright later with the fire and low night-light, and he'd ached to creep into her bed and touch every part of her body with his lips and the tips of his fingers. Teresa was now walking very fast ahead on her own, as if she was ashamed, and he was beginning to desire too.

Then he shuddered as the vision of the farm animals coupling came again, his father doing that to his mother years ago, out of which he'd come, her body in the clay of Aughoo now with worms and the roots of dandelions, and his father rubbing his belly now in the nights in the iron bed with the broken brass bells.

"Our Father, who art in Heaven, hallowed be thy name; thy kingdom come: thy will be done on earth," broke suddenly on his lips as he gathered himself to catch up with the girl so as not to have to come into the village on his own.

Christmas

As well as a railway ticket they gave me a letter before I left the Home to work for Moran. They warned me to give the letter unopened to Moran, which was why I opened it on the train; it informed Moran that since I was a ward of state if I caused trouble or ran away he was to contact the police at once. I tore it up, since it occurred to me that I might well cause trouble or run away, resolving to say I lost it if asked, but Moran did not ask for any letter.

Moran and his wife treated me well. The food was more solid than at the Home, a roast always on Sundays, and when the weather grew hard they took me to the town and bought me Wellingtons and an overcoat and a cap with flaps that came down over the ears. After the day's work when Moran had gone to the pub, I was free to sit at the fire, while Mrs. Moran knitted, and listen to the wireless—what I enjoyed most were the plays—and Mrs. Moran had told me she was knitting me a pullover for Christmas. Sometimes she asked me about life at the Home and when I'd tell her she'd sigh, "You must be very glad to be with us instead," and I would tell her, which was true, that I was. I mostly went to bed before Moran came from the pub as they often quarrelled then, and I considered I had no place in that part of their lives.

Moran made his living by buying cheap branches, or uncommercial timber the sawmills couldn't use, and cutting them up to sell as firewood. I delivered the timber with an old jennet Moran had bought from the tinkers; the jennet squealed, a very human squeal, any time a fire of branches was lit and ran, about the only time he did run, to stand in rigid contentment with his nostrils in the thick of the wood smoke. When Moran was in good humour it amused him greatly to light a fire specially to see the jennet's excitement at the prospect of smoke.

There was no reason this life shouldn't have gone on for long but for a stupid wish on my part, which set off an even more stupid wish in Mrs. Grey, and what happened has struck me ever since as usual when people look to each other for their happiness or whatever it is called. Mrs. Grey was Moran's best customer. She'd come from America and built the huge house on top of Mounteagle after her son had been killed in aerial combat over Italy.

The thaw overhead in the bare branches had stopped, the evening we filled that load for Mrs. Grey; there was no longer the dripping on the dead leaves, the wood clamped in the silence of white frost except for the racket some bird made in the undergrowth. Moran carefully built the last logs above the crates of the cart and I threw him the bag of hay that made the load look bigger than it was. "Don't forget to call at Murphy's for her paraffin," he said. "No, I'll not forget." "She's bound to tip you well this Christmas. We could use money for the Christmas." He'd use it to pour drink down his gullet. "Must be time to be moving," I said. "It'll be night before you're there," he answered.

The cart rocked over the roots between the trees, cold
steel of the bridle ring in the hand close to the rough black
lips, steam of the breath wasting on the air to either side.
We went across the paddocks to the path round the lake,
the wheels cutting two tracks on the white stiff grass, crush
of the grass yielding to the iron. I had to open the wooden
gate to the pass. The small shod hooves wavered between
the two ridges of green inside the wheeltracks on the pass
as the old body swayed to each drive of the shafts, as the
wheels fell from rut to rut.

The lake was frozen over, a mirror fouled by white
blotches of the springs, and rose streaks from the sun
impaled on the firs of Oakport across the bay.

The chainsaw started up in the wood again, he'd saw
while there was light. "No joke to make a living, a drink
or two for some relief, all this ballsing. May be better if we
stayed in bed, conserve our energy, eat less," but in spite of
all he said he went on buying the branches cheap from
McAnnish after the boats had taken the trunks down the
river to the mill.

I tied the jennet to the chapel gate and crossed to
Murphy's shop.

"I want Mrs. Grey's paraffin."

The shop was full of men, they sat on the counter or on
wooden fruit boxes and upturned buckets along the walls.
They used to trouble me at first: I supposed it little different
from going into a shop in a strange country without its
language, but they learned they couldn't take a rise out of
me, that was their phrase. They used to lob tomatoes at the
back of my head in the hope of some reaction, but they left
me mostly alone when they saw none was forthcoming. If

I felt anything for them it was a contempt tempered by fear:
and I was here, and they were there.

"You want her paraffin, do you? I know the paraffin I'd
give her if I got your chance," Joe Murphy said from the
centre of the counter where he presided, and a loyal guffaw
rose from around the walls.

"Her proper paraffin," someone shouted, and it drew
even more applause, and when it died a voice asked,
"Before you get off the counter, Joe, throw us an orange?"
They bought chocolate and fruit as token payment for
their stay. Joe stretched to the shelf and threw the orange
to the man who sat on a bag of Spanish onions. As he
stretched forward to catch the fruit the red string bag col-
lapsed and he came heavily down on the onions, "You
want to bruise those onions with your dirty awkward arse.
Will you pay for them now, will you?" Joe shouted as he
swung his thick legs down from the counter. "Everybody's
out for their onions these days," the man tried to defend
himself with a nervous laugh as he fixed the string bag
upright and changed his seat to an orange box.

"You've had your onions: now pay for them."

"Make him pay for his onions," they shouted.

"You must give her her paraffin first." Joe took the tin,
and went to the barrel raised on flat blocks in the corner,
and turned the copper tap.

"Now give her the proper paraffin. It's Christmas time,"
Joe said again as he screwed the cap tight on the tin, the
limp black hair falling across the bloated face.

"Her proper paraffin," the approving cheer followed me
out the door.

"He never moved a muscle, the little fucker. Those

Homeboys are a bad piece of work," I heard with much satisfaction as I stowed the tin of paraffin securely among the logs of the cart. Ice, over the potholes of the road, was catching the first stars. Lights of bicycles, it was a confession night, hesitantly approached out of the night. Though exposed in the full glare of their lamps I was unable to recognize the bicyclists as they peddled past in dark shapes behind their lamps and this made raw the fear I'd felt but had held down in the shop. I took a stick and beat the reluctant jennet into pulling the load uphill as fast as he was able.

After I'd stacked the logs in the fuel shed I went and knocked on the back door to see where they wanted me to put the paraffin. Mrs. Grey opened the door.

"It's the last load until after Christmas," I said as I put the tin down.

"I haven't forgotten." She smiled and held out a pound note.

"I'd rather not take it." It was there the first mistake was made, playing for higher stakes.

"You must have something, besides the firewood you've brought us so many messages from the village that we don't know what we'd have done without you."

"I don't want money."

"Then what would you like me to give you for Christmas?"

"Whatever you'd prefer to give me." I thought *prefer* was well put for a Homeboy.

"I'll have to give it some thought then," she said as I led the jennet out of the yard delirious with stupid happiness.

"You got the paraffin and logs there without trouble?" Moran beamed when I came in to the smell of hot food. He'd changed into good clothes and was finishing his meal at the head of the big table in tired contentment.

"There was no trouble," I answered.

"You've fed and put in the jennet?"

"I gave him crushed oats."

"I bet you Mrs. Grey was pleased."

"She seemed pleased."

He'd practically his hand out. "You got something good out of it then?"

"No."

"You mean to say she gave you nothing?"

"Not tonight but maybe she will before Christmas."

"Maybe she will but she always gave a pound with the last load before," he said suspiciously. His early contentment was gone.

He took his cap and coat to go for a drink or two for some relief.

"If there's an international crisis in the next few hours you know where I'll be found," he said to Mrs. Moran as he left.

Mrs. Grey came Christmas Eve with a large box. She smelled of scent and gin and wore a fur coat. She refused a chair saying she'd to rush, and asked me to untie the red twine and paper.

A toy airplane stood inside the box, it was painted white and blue and the tyres smelled of new rubber.

"Why don't you wind it up and see it go?"

I looked up at the idiotically smiling face, the tear-brimmed eyes.

"Wind it up for Mrs. Grey," I heard Moran's voice.

While the horrible hurt of the toy was changing to rage I was able to do nothing. Moran took the toy from my hand and wound it up. A light flashed on and off on the tail as it raced across the cement and the propellors turned.

"It was too much for you to bring," Moran said in his politic voice.

"I thought it was rather nice when he refused the money. My own poor boy loved nothing better than model airplanes for Christmas," she was again on the verge of tears.

"We all still feel for that tragedy," Moran said and insisted, "Thank Mrs. Grey for such a lovely present. It's far too good."

"I think it's useless," I could no longer hold back rage, and began to sob. I have only a vague memory afterwards except the voice of Moran accompanying her to the door with excuses and apologies.

"I should have known better than to trust a Homeboy," Moran said when he came back. "Not only did you do me out of the pound but you go and insult the woman and her dead son. You're going to make quick time back to where you came from, my tulip."

Moran stirred the airplane with his boot as if he wished to kick it but dared not out of respect for the money it had cost.

"Well you'll have a good flight in it this Christmas."

The two-hour bell went for Midnight Mass, and as Moran hurried for the pub to get drinks before Mass, Mrs. Moran started to strip the windows of curtains and to set a single candle to burn in each window. Later, as we made our way to the church, candles burned in the windows of all the houses and the church was ablaze with light. I was ashamed of the small old woman, afraid they'd identify me with her, as we walked up between the crowded benches to where a steward directed us to a seat in the women's side-altar. In the smell of burning wax and flowers and damp stone, I got out the brown beads and the black prayerbook with the gold cross on the cover they'd given me in the Home and began to prepare for the hours of boredom Midnight Mass meant; but it did not turn out that way, it was to be a lucky Christmas. A drunken policeman, Guard Mullins, had slipped past the stewards on guard at the door and into the women's sidechapel. As Mass began he started to tell the school-teacher's wife how available her arse had been for handling while she'd worked in the bar before assuming the fur coat of respectability, "And now, O lordy me a prize rose garden wouldn't get a luk in edgeways with its grandeur." The stewards had a hurried consultation whether to eject him or not and decided it'd probably cause less scandal to leave him as he was. They seemed right for he quietened into a drunken stupor until the Monsignor climbed into the pulpit to begin his annual hour of the season of peace and glad tidings. As soon as he began, "In the name of the Father and of the Son and of the Holy Ghost. This Christmas, my dearly beloved children in Christ, I wish . . ." Mullins woke to applaud with a hearty, "Hear, hear. I couldn't approve more. You're a man after my own heart. Down with the hypocrites!" The Monsignor looked towards the policeman and then at the stewards, but as he was greeted by another, "Hear, hear!" he closed his notes and in a voice of acid wished everybody a holy and happy Christmas, and angrily climbed from the pulpit to conclude the shortest Midnight Mass the church had ever known. It was not, though, the end of the entertainment. As the communicants came from the rails Mullins singled out the tax collector, who walked down the aisle with eyes closed, bowed head, and hands rigidly joined, to shout, "There's the biggest hypocrite in the parish," which delighted almost everybody.

I thought of Mullins as my friend as I went past the lighted candles in the window, and felt for the first time proud to be a ward of state. I avoided Moran and his wife and from the attic I listened with glee to them criticizing Mullins. When the voices died I came quietly down to take a box of matches and the airplane and go to the jennet's stable. I gathered dry straw in a heap and as I lit it and the smoke rose he gave his human squeal until I untied him and he was able to put his nostrils in the thick of the smoke. By the light of the burning straw I put the blue and white toy against the wall and started to kick. Each kick I gave, it seemed a new sweetness was injected into my blood. For such a pretty toy it took few kicks to reduce it to shapelessness, and then in the last flames of the straw I jumped on it on the stable floor where the jennet was already nosing me to put more straw on the dying fire.

I was glad, as I quietened, that I'd torn up in the train the letter that I was supposed to give unopened to Moran. I felt a new life for me had already started to grow out of the ashes, out of the stupidity of human wishes.

Hearts of Oak and Bellies of Brass

"If Jocko comes today I'll warm his arse for this once,"
Murphy laughed fiercely; the hair on the powerful arms
that held the sledge was smeared to the skin with a paste of
dust and oil. The small blue eyes twinkled in the leather of
the face as they searched for the effect of what he'd said.
There was always the tension he might break loose from
behind the mixer with the sledge, or if he didn't that
someone else would with shovel or with sledge.

"A disgrace, worse than an animal," Keegan echoed; he
wore a brown hat that stank with sweat and dust over his
bald head. What he was proudest of in the world was that
he had a second cousin who was a schoolmaster in Mohill.

"I want to be at no coroner's inquest on his head,"
Murphy said and started to beat the back of the steel hopper
out of boredom as the engine idled over.

Jocko came every day, crazed on meths and rough cider,
and usually made straight for the pool of shade and water
under the mixer.

"He'd be just a ham sandwich if you brought down the
hopper with him lying there and we'd be all in the fukken
soup," Murphy continued.

"Likes of him coming on the site anyhow would give it
a bad name in no time," Keegan tiraded, while Galway

rested on his shovel, watching the breasts of the machinists lean above their sewing in the third-floor windows of Rose and Margols, gown manufacturers on Christian Street. Galway was youngest of us all. I'd worked the whole of the hot summer with Galway and Keegan behind the mixer Murphy drove like some royal ape, and in the last two weeks Jocko had come every day. The mixer idled away. On the roof they were changing the bays.

"Talkin' about given the site a bad name the way you came in this morning was disgrace to the livin' daylight," Keegan said to me.

"I wouldn't lose any sleep about it if I were you," and my grip tightened on the handle of the shovel, its blade was sharp and silver from a summer of gravel and of sand.

"I come in with a decent jacket and tie, and then I change, I don't come in with work clothes on; if people see you looking like shit they'll take you for shit. I don't know and I don't care what the king of the monkeys wears but we who are Irish should always be tidy when we sit down to tea," he quoted in support out of some forgotten schoolbook.

"You and your fucking monkeys," I said as I kept a tight grip on the shovel as I thought of the lightning change of the face from its ordinary foolishness to viciousness when in horseplay Galway had knocked off the hat to betray the baldness, the blade of the shovel that had just missed Galway's throat.

"King of the fukken monkeys," Galway guffawed as a breast leaned out of sight above her machine, but before Keegan's attack had time to change to Galway, Barney whistled from the scaffolding rail on the roof. The bay was ready. The mixer, in smoke and stink of diesel, roared in gear.

"Come on: shovel or shite; shite or burst," Murphy shouted above the roar.

The shovels drove and threw in time into the long wooden box, tipped by handles at each end into the steel hopper when full, two boxes of gravel to the one of sand, and as the sand was tipped on the gravel Keegan came running from the stack with a cement bag on his shoulder to throw it down on top. Galway's shovel cut the bag in two and the grey cloud of fallout drifted away as the ends were pulled free.

The hopper rose, we could rest on shovels for this minute. When it stopped Murphy took the sledge to beat the back of the hopper, and the last of the sticking sand or gravel ran into the revolving drum where the water sloshed against the blades.

As he hammered he shouted in time, "Our fukker who art in heaven bought his boots for nine-and-eleven," the back of the hopper bright as beaten silver in the sun from a summer's sledging.

As the hopper came down again he shouted in the same time, "Shovel or shite: shite or burst," and the shovels mechanically drove and threw, two boxes of gravel to one of sand, and the grey fallout from the hundredweight of cement as the bag was cut in two and the ends pulled free. It'd go on as this all day.

Murphy ran the mixed concrete from the drum down a shoot into a metal bucket. With a whine of the lift engine the bucket rose to Sligo, a red-faced old man with a cap worn back to front, who tipped it into a cylindrical metal

D

container fixed to the scaffolding, and then ran the bucket down again. The barrows were filled from a trapdoor in the container, and they ran on planks to toss the concrete on the steel in the bays. The best of the roof on a hot day was that wind blew from the Thames there.

In the boredom of the shovelfuls falling in time into the wooden box I start to go over my first day on this site a summer before. They'd said to roll my jacket in the gutter before I went in, and when I did to ask for the *shout*.

"Who has the *shout* here?" I'd asked. They'd pointed Barney out, he wore the same black mourning suit in Wellingtons that he now leaned in against the scaffolding rail, watching the concreting on the roof, the black tie hanging loose from the collar of the dirty white shirt.

"Any chance of a start?" I'd asked as they said to ask.

His eyes went over me—shoulders, arms, thighs. I remembered my father's cattle I had stood for sale in the Shambles once, walking stick along the backbone to gauge the rump, lips pulled back to read the teeth, but then I was offering to shovel for certain shillings an hour: shovel or shite; shite or burst in the ears each mixing.

"Have you ever done any building work before?" Barney had asked.

"No but I've worked on land," they'd said not to lie.

"What kind of work?"

"The usual—turf, oats, potatoes."

"You've just come over on the boat then?"

"Yesterday . . . and I heard you might give me the start."

"Start at twelve then," he said in his slow way and pointed to the wooden hut that was the office. "They'll give you the address of the Labour there, and get back with your cards before twelve."

There was no boredom those first days, though time was slower and more pain, drive to push the shovel in blistered hands with raw knee in the same time as the others, a shovel slyly jabbed against your thigh as if you've stumbled in the way and the taunt, "Too much wankin' that's what's wrong," in the way fowl will peck to death a weakened hen; fear of Thursday, Barney's tap on the shoulder, "You're not strong enough for this job. You'll have to look for something lighter for yourself. Your cards'll be ready in the office at payout." No fear of the tap on the shoulder on this or any Thursday now, shut mouth and patience and the hardening of the body so that the shovel drove and threw as mechanically as theirs had worn the attack away.

"What time is it?" I asked Keegan. He fumbled in his pocket for the big silver watch wrapped in cloth to protect it against the dust. He read the time.

"Another fukken twenty minutes to go," Galway said in the exasperation of the burden of the slow passing of the minutes, a coin for each endured minute.

"Another fukken twenty minutes," I repeated, the re-petitious use of fukken with every simple phrase came harsh at first and now a habit, its omission here would cause as much unease as its use where "Very kind. Thank you, Mr. Jones" was demanded.

"There's no fukken future in this job," Keegan com-plained tiredly. "You get old. The work is the same, but you're less able for it anymore. In other jobs as you get old you can put the work over on others."

"No sign of Jocko yet," Galway tried to change to Murphy. Galway wore a white handkerchief knotted at both ends to keep the dust out of his Brylcreemed black hair.

"I'll give him his future when he comes," Murphy said as he sledged the back of the hopper.

"The childer go to school and they'll have better than me," Keegan kept on at what was felt as nagging rebuke. "They'll have some ambition. That's why I work behind this bloody mixer and the woman chars. So that they can go to school. They'll have some ambition. They'll wear white collars."

"Pork chops, pints of bitter, and a good old ride before you sleep, that's fukken ambition," Murphy left off sledging to shout, and when he finished he laughed above the mixer.

"That's right," Galway agreed. "Come on, Keegan: shovel."

"I'll shovel with a jumpedup brat anyday," Keegan answered with the same antagonism but fell behind, sweat running down from under the hat.

"Shovel or shite: shite or burst," Murphy trumpeted as he saw the competition, and then at last the hooter blew.

We passed the Negro demolition crew as we went to the canteen, the wood from the houses burning fiercely behind the bulldozer, and on the roof two Negroes hacked away the slates with pickaxes. The prostitutes lived in the condemned row, moving from empty house to empty house ahead of the demolition, limp rubbers in the gutters Monday mornings while they slept in the daylight.

Through the hatch in the canteen Marge handed out ham or tomato rolls and mugs of tea.

"Ta ta, Pa," she said as I gave her coins and this had been hardest of all to get used to, to have no name at all easier than to be endlessly called *Pa*.

"Thanks, Marge"; and it angered me that there was the bitterness of irony still in my smile, that I was not yet completely my situation; this ambition of mine in reverse, to annul all the votes in myself.

I sat with the rest of the mixer gang at a trestle table. Behind us the chippies played cards. The enmity still sullenly glowed between Galway and Keegan but Galway ate his rolls and gulped tea without lifting his head from the racing paper, where he marked his fancies with a stub of pencil.

I read aloud out of the local *Herald* my mother sent me each week from home that prayers had been ordered in all the churches in Ireland for good weather, it had rained all summer, and now the harvest was in danger.

"That it may rise higher than for fukken Noah. That they may have to climb trees," Murphy answered, laughing, vicious.

"They never did much for us except to starve us out to England. You have to have the pull there or you're dirt," Keegan advanced.

The familiar tirade would continue, predictable as the drive and throw of their shovels, and I went outside to sit on a stack of steel in the sun until the hooter blew, but even there it wasn't possible to be alone, for Tipperary followed to sit too on the steel. He'd been taken away to the Christian Brothers when he was eleven, but hadn't been able to pass the exams that would have qualified him a teacher, and when they put him to work in the kitchens he'd left and come to England. He fixed steel in the bays. The cheeks were hollow, infantile puzzlement on the regular face from which sensuality if it had ever been there had withered.

"Do you think Shakespeare's all he's bumped up to be?" he asked. He'd heard that I'd gone two years to Secondary School, and he believed that he and me could speak as one educated man to another: he was sometimes called the *Professor*, and baited mercilessly, though there was a purity in his dogged stupidity that troubled them towards a certain respect; but his attention made me uncomfortable, I had no desire to be one of his thieves at these occasional crucifixions, or to play Judas for them to his Christ.

I told him that I didn't know if Shakespeare was all that he was bumped up to be, but people said so, and it was people who did all the bumping up or bumping down.

"But who is people?" he pursued.

"People is people. They praise Shakespeare. Pull your beer. Give you the start. They might even be ourselves."

I laughed, and watched the door of the canteen, and listened for the hooter, and longed to hurt him away: he touched something deeper than my careful neutrality. And I hadn't the strength to live by anything deeper.

"And do you consider George Bernard Shaw all that he's bumped up to be?" he asked, puzzling over and over perhaps his failure to answer satisfactorily the questions they'd put to him at the exams before they'd sent him to the kitchens.

"I know nothing about George Bernard." I got up off the steel.

"But you went to Secondary School?"

"For two years."

"But why didn't you go on? You passed the exams."

"Forget it. I didn't go on. I've never regretted it," I was disturbed, and resented it, and hated Tipperary for the disturbance.

"But why, you'd have learned things? You'd have learned whether things are what they're bumped up to be or not."

"I'd have learned nothing. I might have got a better job but my ambition is wrong way round anyhow. Almost as good behind the mixer as anywhere else."

While Tipperary meditated a next question there was a motionless silence between us on the stack of rusted steel in the sun.

"Murphy says he's going to do Jocko if he comes today," I changed.

"Sligo has some plans, too, up top," he answered slowly. "It's not fair."

"It'll happen though—if he comes."

The hooter blew. Nobody came from the canteen. They'd sit there till Barney stormed in. "Come on. You don't get paid sittin' on your arses five minutes after the hooter's gone. Come on. Out."

"How's it going, Paddy Boy?" the lorry driver asked as he got me to sign for the load of gravel he'd tipped behind the mixer.

"Dragging along," I answered as I scrawled a few illegible letters on the docket, it never mattered who signed.

"Keep it going, that's it," he touched my shoulder before turning to shout a few friendly obscenities at Murphy who'd started the mixer.

The heat grew worse, Jocko didn't come, nobody spoke

much, even on Galway's face sweat ran down to streak the white coating of cement dust.

"Anyone volunteer to go for lemonade?" Keegan asked when more than an hour had gone. I said I'd go to Greenbaum's, it was some minutes escape from the din of the engines and diesel and dust in the airless heat.

"Walkin' kills me these days," Keegan was grateful.

I went through the gap in the split stakes linked with wire into Hessell Street, green and red peppers among the parsley and fruit of the stalls; it smelled of lice and blood and fowl, down and feathers stamped into the blood and henshit outside the Jewish poulterers, country air after the dust of the mixer.

"Six Tizers," I asked Greenbaum, old grey Jew out of Poland. "Put them on the slate."

"Everything on the slate, and then one day you jack and go, and Greenbaum is left with the baby."

"You'll get paid. Today is payday."

"And Greenbaum charges no deposit on the bottles. You just throw them away. And who loses? Greenbaum loses," he complained as he put the bottles on the counter, as much in love with complaint as the cripple with the crutches he goes on using after he is cured.

The bottles were passed around from mouth to mouth behind the mixer as the bucket climbed to Sligo at the top.

"You shouldn't gurgle," Keegan ragged at Galway. "We who are Irish——"

"Should always be tidy when we sit down to tea," Galway took up viciously. "Come on: shovel, you old bollocks."

"Shovel or shite: shite or burst. It's payday," Murphy

shouted as if *shovel* had set an alarm off in his head, and without break the shovels drove and threw, two boxes of gravel to one of sand, the small grey puff of cement in the airless heat as we pulled the cut ends of the bag loose, till the hooter blew for payout.

Tipperary joined me at the end of the queue outside the payout window.

"Jocko didn't arrive yet," I said to keep his conversation easy.

"No. Sligo's going to put the water on him from up top when he comes. It's not fair."

"It'll probably happen though."

"But it's not fair."

We each held the thin brass medal on which our number was stamped, a hole in the medal for hanging it on the nail in the hut at night.

At the window we called our name and number and showed the brass medal and the timekeeper handed us our pay in a small brown packet.

On the front of the packet were written the number of hours we had worked, the rate per hour, the amount we'd earned minus the various deductions.

As the men stood around checking their money, the large hands counting awkwardly and slowly, a woman's voice cried, "Come and get them while they're hot."

Their eyes lifted to search for the voice, towards the condemned row of houses ahead of the bulldozer and the burning wood, where from an upper window old Kathleen leaned out, shaking her large loose breasts at the men.

"Cheap at the price," she cried. A cheer went up; and some obscenities were shouted like smallarms fire.

"Even better downstairs," she cried back, her face flushed with alcohol.

"A disgrace. Terrible," Tipperary said.

"It's all right. She just got excited by the money," he disturbed me more than she did.

"This evening after pints of bitter they'll slink round," he said.

As I did once. A Christmas Eve. She'd told me she'd all her Christmas shopping done except her turkey. She'd said she hoped to get one cheap at Smithfield, she said they dropped the prices before the market closed to get rid of the surplus, and she was relying on a customer who was a porter there.

Only for her old practised hands it'd have been impossible to raise desire, and if it was evil when it happened, the pumping of the tension of the instinct into her glycerined hole, then nothing was so extraordinarily ordinary as this evil.

"Why not? Let them go round, and what's so fuckign special about what's between your legs anyhow?" I shouted at him, and turned my back so as not to have to see the hurt on this dim acolyte's face in its confusion of altars. I started to count out the money from the small brown packet.

I love to count out in money the hours of my one and precious *life*. I sell the hours and I get money. The money allows me to sell more hours. If I saved money I could buy the hours of some similar bastard and live like a royal incubus, which would suit me much better than as I am now, though apparently even as I am now suits me well enough, since I do not want to die.

Full of beer that night after the *Rose and Crown* we went round to Marge and Kathleen like dying elephants in the condemned row. Before I'd finished counting, Tipperary timidly tapped my shoulder and I shouted, "Fuck off," and did not turn to see his face

The hooter went. The offered breasts withdrew. A window slammed.

"The last round," someone said.

The mixer started. The shovels drove and threw: gravel, sand, gravel; gravel, sand, gravel; cement.

Murphy sledged on the beaten steel of the hopper, vocal again that the brown packet was a solid wad against his arse. "Our fukker who art in heaven bought his boots for nine-and-eleven," he sang out as he sledged. "Come on: shovel or shite; shite or burst."

Jocko came so quietly that he was in the pool of shadow under the hopper before he was noticed, the pint bottle of violet-coloured spirit swinging wide from one pocket, crawling on all fours towards the pool of water in the sand beneath the drum of the mixer.

"Out," Murphy shouted with a curse, angered Jocko had got so far without being noticed. "Out. I'll teach your arse a lesson. Out."

He took the shovel that leaned against the mixer, and drove at Jocko, the dull thud of the blade on cloth and flesh or bone, buttocks that someone must have bathed once, carried in her arms.

"I warned you if you tried this stunt again I'd warm your arse. I want to be at no coroner's inquest on your head. Out."

We stood and watched Murphy drive him out of the

pool water, push him out of the shadow of the hopper into the evening glare, we said nothing.

The eyes in the hollow sockets, grey beard matted about the scabs of the face, registered no pain, no anything: and when they fell on the barrow of wet concrete that the surveyor had used to test the strength of the mix he moved mechanically towards it, sat in, and started to souse himself up and down in the liquid concrete as a child in a bath.

"Jesus when that sets to his arse it'll be nobody's business," Galway said between dismay and laughter.

"Out of the fukken barrow," Murphy shouted, and lifted him out by the neck, pushing him down the tyre-marked yellow slope. He staggered but did not fall. The wet clothes clung to his back and the violet-coloured bottle in the pocket was clouded and dirty with wet concrete.

Sligo, the cap back to front, leaned across the scaffolding rail on top, the black rubber hose in his hands. The jet of water started to circle Jocko, darkening the yellow sand. Sligo used his thumb on the jet so that it sprayed out much as heavy rain.

When Jocko first felt the water he lifted his face to its coolness but then, slow and deliberate, he took a plastic coat and faded beret from the opposite pocket to where the bottle swung and in the same slow deliberate way put them on, buttoning the plastic coat to the throat and putting the collar up.

The jet followed a few yards of his slow walk and then fell back but he still walked in the evening sun as if it was raining.

Greenbaum, old grey rat searching for Tizer bottles

among the heaps of rubble, lifted his head to watch him pass through the gap in the fence of split stakes into Hessell Street but immediately bent again to search and complain, "Greenbaum charges no deposit on the bottles, and then what do they do, throw them away, throw them away, never return. Greenbaum's an old fool."

Strandhill, The Sea

The street in front of Parkes' Guest House; grains of sand
from the street coming on the grey fur of the tennis ball,
the hopping under my hand idle as the conversations from
the green bench before the flowerbed, red bells of the
fuchsia vivid behind them and some roses and gilly-
flowers, the earth around the roots of everything speckled
with sea shells, overhead the weathered roughcast of the
wall of the house.

The sky was filling. Rain would come, and walls close
around the living evening; looking towards the bleared
windows, no way to get out from the voices.

"There was great stuff in those Baby Fords and Austins.
The cars going nowadays are only tin compared," Mr.
McVittie said, the heavy gold watch chain across the waist-
coat of the brown suit, silver hair parted in the centre,
knobbed walking stick in his hand; as if out of a yellowed
wedding photo.

"Only they weren't so fast as now," Mr. O'Connor
added, following McVittie all the week in the way stray
dogs at night will stick to any pair of heels that seem to go
home.

"Before the war, before I got married, I used to have one
of the old Citroens, and it could go forever, only it was

very hard on petrol," Mr. Ryan said, feel of his eyes on the up and down of the tennis ball on the street.

Conversations always the same: height of the Enfield rifle, summer of the long dresses, miles to the gallon—from morning to the last glows of the cigarettes on the benches at night, always informations, informations about every-things, having come out of darkness now blinking with informations at all the things about them, before the soon when they'll have to leave.

The sky filled over Sligo Bay, the darkness moving across the links and church, one clear strip of blue between Parkes' and Knocknarea, and when that'd fill—the rain, the steamed windows, the informations till the dark settled on their day.

Fear of the sky since morning had kept them on the benches away from the strand a mile downhill they'd come to enjoy, fear of the long trudge past the Golf Links and Kincora and Central in rain; but they'd still the air here, sea air, it was some consolation. Even the strand, reached in good weather, the mile downhill accomplished, the mile home uphill yet out of mind, and in possession of strand of Strandhill, long and level for miles, the cannon on its rot-ting initial-covered carriage pointed towards the Atlantic as if on guard over the two ice-cream parlours; women at the tideline, with a child in one hand and skirt held tight between thighs with the other, whinnying at each spent rush of water at their feet before it curled in a brown backwash round their heels; all this time envy of the buckets and beach ball of others to gladden a royal stay.

Cars ran miles to the gallon, still on the bench: 25, 32, 39 with careful timing and more use of clutch than brake.

Another guest, Mr. Haydon, marked the racing columns of the newspaper on the edge of the same bench; hairnet of purple threads on the face, commercial traveller. "Never made the grade," McVittie had pronounced. "Soon for the jump." On the next bench a pattern for a fairisle pullover lay open between Mrs. O'Connor and Mrs. Ryan, and around them children in all postures. Ingolsby was the one guest who sat alone, retired lecturer of English, while the tennis ball hopped or paused.

"What part of the world is Lagos in?" Haydon stirred out of the newspaper to interrupt the wear and tear on clutches. "You should know that, Mr. Ryan. You're a teacher."

"I think Africa," the uncertain reply came, and his sudden flush and paling brought Ingolsby in.

"Because somebody happens to be a teacher is no reason why they should know where Lagos is."

"If teachers don't know that sort of thing who can know?" Haydon was angered. "Don't they have to teach the stuff to kids?"

"If a teacher has to teach a geography lesson he simply looks up his information in a textbook beforehand. A doctor doesn't go round with all his patients' ailments in his head. He has files." Ingolsby explained with solid satisfaction.

"But it's not getting us any nearer to where the hell Lagos is?"

"It's in Nigeria," Ingolsby said.

"It's in Nigeria, in Africa," Ryan tried to smooth over the antagonism.

"That was what I wanted to know. Thank you, Mr.

Ryan," Haydon said pointedly and buried his head in the newspaper again.

"Amazing the actual number of places there is in this world, when you come to think," O'Connor added.

"A man could spend his whole life learning the names of places and they'd still be as many as the sands of the seashore left," McVittie said.

The ball was idle in hand. The tide was full, a coal boat moving out from Sligo in the channel. There were no blue spaces against Knocknarea.

Small annual calvary of the poor, mile downhill and uphill between Parkes' and the cannon. The Calm Sea closer, inlet that ran to Ballisodare past the lobster pool, no envy there, deserted except the one day they put flags down and held the races at low tide, but still in the dead quiet the pain of voices coming across the golf links, and Jane Simpson with others there.

The first rain was loud on Haydon's newspaper, and it was followed by a general rising and gradual procession indoors between the still sparse drops.

"Imagine the name they called this," Ingolsby paused to hold a blood-orange rose towards Ryan as they went along the flowerbed.

"I'm not so well up on flowers," Ryan apologized.

"*Climbing Mrs. Sam McGredy. Climbing Mrs. Sam Mc-Gredy*," Ingolsby enunciated.

"Names are a funny thing," Ryan said without thought.

"Names are a funny thing, as you put it," Ingolsby repeated sarcastically. "*Peace* or *Ena Harkness* or even the *Moulin Rouge* but *Climbing Mrs. Sam McGredy*. That's an atom bomb," and then he lowered his voice. "Never feel

E

you have to know anything because you happen to teach. Never let them bully you with their assumptions of what you should be. Say you don't know, that it can be discovered in books, if they're interested. It's only pretending to know something that's embarrassing."

The counsel roused impotent deeps of hatred in Ryan's eyes as they went the last steps to the door.

A Miss Evans was the one addition to the company over lunch, and when the litter of that was cleared away with the sheets that served as cloth, and the old varnish of the big elliptical table shone dully about the bowl of roses put back on its centre, Mrs. Parkes set a small coal fire to burn in the grate almost as some apology for the gloom of rain; and all the bars of the evening had fallen into place. "The rain anywhere is bad but at the sea, at the sea, it's the end," rose as a constant sighing in the conversations.

The need to escape to some other world grew fiercer but there was no money. "Steal, steal, steal," was the one way out.

Raincoat and southwester and outside without them noticing. Mist half-way down the slopes of Knocknarea, rain and mist blurring the sea. Past Huggards, past the peeling white swan sailing on the signboard of the Swan Hotel, steady drip from the eaves louder than the distant fall of the sea and gull cries, glow of the electric light burning inside through the mist on Peebles' window, stationer and confectioner; shock of the warning bell ringing as you opened the door.

A girl in blue overalls behind the counter was helping a man choose postcards and they were laughing.

"Can I help you?" she turned.

"I want to look round," it was the only possible thing, and it was luck she was busy with the man.

Rows of comics were on the counter, hours of insensibility to the life in Parkes', *Wizard* and *Hotspur* and *Rover* and *Champion*, whole worlds.

Put a *Hotspur* on top of the *Wizard*, both on top of the yellow pile of Rovers, and draw breath. The man was paying for the postcards. Lift the three free, put them inside the open raincoat, the elbow holding them tight against the side. Walk.

"Any chance of seeing you in the Silver Slipper tonight?" the man asked.

"Stranger things happened in the world," she answered, and they both laughed again.

It was impossible to walk loose and casual to the door, it was one forced step after the other, having to think to walk, waiting all the time for the blow from behind. "Excuse me," it'd probably begin, and then the shame, the police. To get caught the one reason not to steal. In the next world it was only a venial sin, purgatory, and the saints alone got the through express to heaven.

Step after step and rigid step and no blow, a cash register ringing and then the warning bell above the door, and the breathing relief of the wet out-of-doors to the sea blurred beyond the golf links, rain coming down same as ever before. Past Huggards and over the sodden sand of the street, raindrops brilliant in the red ruffles of the roses by the wall.

"Where did you get the money from for that trash?" came once I was in the room.

"Sixpence I found down at the front yesterday."

"Why have you to be always stuck in that trash? Why can't you read something good like Shakespeare that'll be of some use to you later?"

The old tune: some use to you later.

"I don't imagine the comics'll do much harm. Good taste isn't cultivated in a day. We rise on stepping stones to greater things," Ingolsby intervened.

"I suppose there's some consolation in that," Ryan was anxious to escape, knowing the hostility the themes of Ingolsby's ponderous conversations roused, they were felt as a slur or rebuke, but he'd not easily escape, Ingolsby needed to live through his own voice too this wet evening.

"What's your opinion of Shakespeare's validity for the modern world?"

"It's not so easy to say," he deferred again, his eyes anxious about the room, his wife on the sofa with Mrs. O'Connor, measuring a sleeve of a pullover on their daughter; soon she'd be knitting silently and patiently again while the night came the same as every other coming into her patient life, while McVittie said to O'Connor:

"The shops out in the country were hard hit by emigration. But we managed to survive. We branched into new lines. We got Esso to put down a petrol pump for instance. We changed with the times."

"It's a cardinal law of nature that every man should have his head firmly screwed on to know how to change with the times and survive," O'Connor agreed.

The people in the room had broken up into their separate groups, and when Miss Evans raised her arms in a yawn out of the chair Haydon leaned forward to say, "There must have been right old sport last night."

"I beg your pardon, Mr. Haydon," she laughed pleased.

"The way all women are, all on their dignity till the business gets down to brass tacks and then an almighty turn of events. And who'd object to an old roll between the sandhills after the dancing anyhow?" he raised his voice, as if to irritate Ingolsby, who was pressing a reluctant Ryan on Wordsworth.

She laughed softly, a hint of defiance against the unconcealed hostility of the married women with their children in the laugh, smiling a little as she looked towards the windows streaming with rain.

"The sandhills won't be much of a temptation tonight, Mr. Haydon."

"No," he said, laughing gently with her, "but where there's an old will there's always an old way." And in a voice gentle with what seemed regret he inquired, "It was at the Silver Slipper you were last night, wasn't it, a bird told me?"

"The bird was right," she said. "The Blue Aces were playing there."

"The rain, the rain at the sea, is deadly," he turned absent from her on some tiredness or memory and reached and took a white shell from the mantelpiece and held it to his ear to listen to it roar.

"It makes everything miserable," McVittie said, tired of his complete possession of O'Connor, but all Haydon did was nod heavily as he replaced the shell and turned again to the girl.

The wash of rain on the windows, the light through their mist going dull on the blue sea of the wallpaper, the red and yellow hollyhocks as the tall flowering masts of sailing ships; and when a child wiped a clearing on the glass, cabbages showed between the apple trees in the garden, and the green cooking apples were bright and shining in the leaves with rain.

"Education comes from the Latin *educo*, lead forth. People seemed to have forgotten that in the modern interpretation of education," Ingolsby laboured; some consolation to Ryan that he'd left the poets but his eyes still apologized to the room, he'd make it even clearer yet, in his own time.

The turning of the pages without reading, pleasure of delaying pleasure to come, and heroes filled those pages week after week, Rockfist Rogan and Alf Tupper and Wilson the Iron Man. The room, the conversations, the cries of the seagulls, the sea, faded, and it was world of imagination, among the performing gods, what I ashamedly desired to become.

Alf Tupper put aside welder and goggles, changed into his country's singlet to leave the whole field standing in that fantastic last lap, and Wilson, *Wilson, the Iron Man, simply came alone into Tibet and climbed to the top of Everest.*

Bomb Box

They cut the tongues out of the dead foxes brought to the barracks and threw them to the grey cat or across the netting wire into the garden. They cut the tongues out of the foxes so that the same fox couldn't be brought back again for the half-crown the government gave for each dead fox in its campaign for the extermination of foxes. Dry mornings they put out the "Recruitment" and "Thistle Ragwort Dock" posters on their boards and took them in again at nightfall and when it rained.

The Sergeant and his policeman, Bannon, had other such duties, for the last crime had been four years before when Mike Moran stole the spare wheel of Guinea McLoughlin's tractor, but as he later threw it in the river they'd not enough evidence to obtain a conviction; so, as an army in peacetime, their main occupation was boredom, though they had similar useless exercises: the Sergeant was supposed to inspect the solitary Bannon on parade at nine each morning; they'd spend a certain number of hours patrolling local roads on their bikes; one or other of them had always to be on BO duty in the day-room beside the phone that seldom rang—and these regulations the superintendent miles away in the town tried to enforce by surprise inspections. These inspections usually found the Sergeant at work in his garden. As he'd almost certainly have been signed out in the books on some fictitious patrol by Bannon, he'd have to run for cover of the trees along the river, and stay hidden there until he'd hear the car leave, when he'd saunter in nervously chewing a grass stalk to ask what had taken place.

All this changed from the day he bought one of the lucky dips at Moroney's auction. The lucky dips were a way to get rid of the junk at the end of the auction. They came in large sugar-bags; his bag concealed two canisters of nuts and bolts and a yellowed medical dictionary.

Now Bannon was sent out on the bike to patrol the local roads or at least write in the book what he did, while the Sergeant sat all day in the day-room poring over the yellowed pages of diseases and their remedies. The weeds in the garden started to choke the young lettuce, the edges of the unsprayed potato leaves to fritter black, and when the summer thunder with its violent showers made the growth more rapid he called me down to the day-room.

"Sit down," he offered a chair by turning it towards the empty fireplace.

The dictionary was open among the foolscap ledgers on the table, *Patrick Moroney MD 1893* in faded purple copperplate on its flyleaf.

"You're old enough to know that nobody can be expected to live for ever?" he began.

"Yes." I didn't know what to answer.

"If you expect something it's only common intelligence to prepare for it, isn't that right?"

"Yes."

"Our ages being what they are, it's no more than natural to expect me to be the first to go?"

"But that'll be years yet."

"We thought that once before and we were wrong. One never knows the day or the hour. The foolish virgins are our lesson."

I sat stiff on the wooden chair.

"If I go you're the oldest and you'll have to look after the others. I think now is the time to begin to learn to fend for yourselves. This summer I expect you to look after the garden and timber as if I no longer existed. That way there'll be no danger you'll be caught napping when the day comes."

"But you do exist," I said bewildered.

"Have I to spell it out," he suddenly shouted, "that as far as the garden and timber goes I won't exist. And I'll see to the best of my ability that you'll learn not to depend on me for ever. It's no more than my Christian duty. Is that clear now?"

"Yes."

"Begin by informing the others of the state of affairs. There has to be some beginning somewhere. Is that clear now?"

"Yes." I left to go up the long hallway to the living quarters, the noise of the children at play on its stone floor growing louder. "I exist, I don't exist" confused in my head as I tried to think of how to tell them the state of affairs, bewildered as to what they were.

They laughed when I tried to explain, and then I shouted, "Shut up, or I'll make you shut up, he said he'd give us no help, that we'd have to learn to do it on our own. No: I'm not answering questions. That's what he said we'd have to do. That is all," and they grew as quiet as I had grown in the day-room.

It took long, tedious days to weed the garden, our hands staining black with the weeds, but there was the excitement of danger in bringing the timber down by boat from Oakport and when the stack grew by the water's edge the Sergeant approved, "The hard way is the only way."

On hot days he sat outside on one of the yellow day-room chairs with the dictionary, the young swallows playing between their clay nests overhead under the drainpipe. The laughter from the garden disturbed him. They were pelting each other with clay. He put down the book to come out where I was backing up the matted furrows, pumping half-canfuls of spray out on the potato stalks.

"It's not enough for you to work. You have to keep an eye on the others as well," he scolded.

"What'll I do if they won't heed?" I asked. I was wet and tired backing up the rows of dripping stalks. I'd more than I was prepared to take.

"Get a stick to them, that's what you'll do," he said and left, anxious to return to the book. "I have to get some peace."

The circuit court saw him in Carrick, and he took home a thermometer in a shining steel case, senna leaves, sulphur, cascara, various white and grey powders, rose-water, and slender glass flagons, in which he began to keep samples of his urine, each morning holding the liquid in the delicate glass to the window light to search for trace of sediment. His walk grew slower and more careful.

From the autumn circuit he brought a cow's head, blood

staining the newspaper; and a bomb box, the colour of grass and mud, war surplus. He showed us how to open the head down its centre, scrape out the brains, cut the glazed eyes out of the sockets and the insides of the black lips with their rubberlike feelers.

Before going to bed we put it to stew over a slow fire. The next morning he remained in bed. He knocked with his shoe on the boards and told us to inform Bannon that he was going sick. After signing the ledgers at nine Bannon climbed the stairs to discover how he was, and on coming down rang Neary, the police doctor. Downstairs I'd to shout the others quiet: "If you bring the Sergeant down he'll murder us."

Neary called on his way to his noon dispensary. Bannon climbed with him to the bedroom door. Only the low murmur of question and answer, the creak of moving shoes on the boards, came at first, but then the voices rose to an incoherent shouting. They lulled again, while the doctor apparently made some additional examination, only to rise again worse than ever. The voices brought Bannon to the open door at the foot of the stairs to listen there with hands behind his back. Each time the voices died he returned to his patient surveyal of the road from the day-room window, only to be brought back to the foot of the stairs by a fresh bout of shouting. He was visibly uneasy, straightening down the front of his tunic, stuffing the white hankie farther up his sleeve, when the bedroom door opened and closed sharply, and the doctor's quick steps were on the stairs. Bannon waited out of sight inside the open doorway until the doctor was at the foot of the stairs, then appeared obsequiously to unbolt the heavy front door of the porch, and followed Neary out on the gravel. The examination had lasted well past the noon of the doctor's dispensary.

"I hope there's nothing serious?" Bannon ventured on the gravel.

"As serious as it can be—apparently mortal," the doctor answered with angry sarcasm as he put his satchel over on the passenger seat of his car. "And he knows all about it. Why he needs to see me is the one puzzlement."

"How long will I mark him in the sick-book for?" Bannon shied away.

"Till kingdom come," the doctor answered; but, before he closed the car door, changed: "Till Wednesday. I'll come on Wednesday."

Until Wednesday we took him broth of the cow's head and milk puddings, the air stale in the room with the one window shut tight on the river and half-blinded; and Bannon, morning and evening, brought him local gossip or report, in which he took no interest. Every hour he spooned a concoction he'd made from the juice of senna leaves and some white powders.

On Wednesday Neary appeared well before his dispensary hour and this time the room upstairs was much quieter, though the door did close on, "What I want is to see a specialist, not a bunch of country quacks," but the doctor seemed more quiet this time as he came down to the waiting Bannon at the foot of the stairs. When they passed through the heavy door on to the gravel, thick-veined sycamore leaves blowing towards the barrack wall from the trees of the avenue, Neary tentatively asked: "Had you noticed any change in the Sergeant before he took to bed?"

"How do you mean, doctor?" Bannon was as always cautious.

"Any changes in his way of going through his normal day?"

"Well, there was the book."

"The book?"

"The book he spent the whole summer poring over, a book he bought at the auction."

"What kind of book?"

"Medical book, it was."

"Medical book," the doctor moved stones of the gravel slowly with his shoe as he repeated, "I might have known. Well, I won't deny him benefit of specialists if that's what he needs," and in the evening the doctor rang that a bed was available in the Depot Hospital. The Sergeant was to travel on the next day's train. A police car or ambulance would meet him off the train at Amiens Street Station.

When Bannon climbed the stairs with the news the Sergeant immediately rose and dressed.

"It took him a long time to see light," was his single comment.

"I hope you won't be long there," the careful answer came.

"Tell the girls to get my new uniform out of the press," he asked the policeman. "And to get shirts and underwear and pyjamas out for packing."

When he came down he told Bannon he could go home: "You'll have to mind this place for long enough on your own. I'll keep an eye on the phone for this evening."

The packing he supervised with great energy, only remembering he was ill late, and then his movements grew slow and careful again, finally shutting himself away with the silent phone behind the day-room door, but before he did, he told me he wanted to see me there after the others had gone to bed.

A low "Come in" answered my knock.

His feet rested on the bricks of the fireplace, a weak heat came from the dying fire of ash, and beside him, on another yellow chair, was the bomb box, the colour of mud and grass. A tin oil-lamp was turned low on the trestle table, on the black and red ink-stains, on the wooden dip pens standing in their wells, on the heavy ledgers and patrol books, on an unsheathed baton. A child muttering in its sleep from the upstairs room came through the door I'd left open. "Shut it. We're not in a field," he said, and I closed it on the now silent house with a shiver.

"Early, in the summer, we talked about you managing without me. And you did a good job in the garden and bringing the timber down. Well, it looks as if we prepared none too soon."

"How?"

"You know what clothes and feeds you all—my pay. The police own the roof above your head. With my death that comes to a full stop. We all know how far your relatives can be depended on—as far as the door."

He'd his greatcoat on over his uniform, the collar turned up but unbuttoned, his shoulders hunched in a luxury of care as if any sudden movement might quench the weak flame of life the body held.

"Fortunately I have made provisions for the day," he said, turning to the bomb box on the chair, and with the same slow carefulness unlocked it. Inside, against the mud and grass camouflage over the steel, was a green wad of money in a rubber band, two brown envelopes and a large package.

"You see this money," he said. "It's £100. That's for the immediate expenses when they take the body home. It won't cross the bridge, it'll go to Aughoo, to lie with your mother, no matter what your relatives try.

"Then open this envelope, it has your name," he lifted the thin brown envelope, "all instructions for the immediate death, what to do, are down there one by one.

"This other envelope has the will and deeds," he continued. "Lynch the solicitor in Boyle has the other copy, and the day after the funeral take this copy into him.

"I have discussed it all with Lynch, he'll help you with the purchase of a small farm, for after the death you'll have to get out of the barracks if you don't all want to be carted off to the orphanage, and if you dither the saved money'll go like snow off a rope. Paddy Mullaney wants to sell and Lynch and I agreed it's ideal if it comes at the right price. After the farm the first thing to get is a cow. "You'll have to work from light to dark on that farm to keep these children but it'll be worth it and you have my confidence."

He locked the box, and handed me one of the keys.

"You have a key and I have a key. When news of the death comes you'll go first thing and open the box with your key. Is that clear?" he demanded, no illness now in the voice.

What was to happen was taking clearer outline as I listened, eyes fixed on the bright metal of the key in the sweat of my palm, but I didn't want to believe. I was too young. Responsibility was for when I grew old.

"The bigger package is not for the time being of any importance. It's for when you grow older. Old watches, your mother's rings, photos, locks of hair, medals, albums, certificates. It's for when you all grow older." In the lull the excitement went, he remembered he was ill, and sank back at once into the dark blue greatcoat.

What he'd been saying was that he was going to die, coffined into the grave, covered over, rot to bones and eaten boards, give no answer to any call, the call given back into the dumbness of my own life on the face of the earth.

Mullaney's farm where we'd go to live, small slated house of the herd, fields sloping uphill to the mound, wet ground about the mound where once they'd startled a hare out of its form in the brown rushes; it had paused in the loop of its flight as the shot blasted its tense listening into a crumpled stillness. Stone walls of those fields.

Drudge of life from morning to night to feed the mouths, to keep the roof above their heads in the heaviness of fifteen years. The ugly and skin shapes of starlings, beaks voracious at the rim of the nest, days grown heavier with the burden of the carrying.

"But you're not going to die."

"All the symptoms point to the one fact that it's certain."

"But the symptoms may be wrong."

"No. It's fairly certain."

"Don't, don't . . ."

"Do you love me then?"

He wanted to see his life in the mirror of the pain of need.

"Yes."

"If you love me then you must do your best for the

others. We can't order our days. They are willed. We have to trust in the mercy of God," he intoned.

"I'll have nobody." I was terrified.

"You have the key. You'll open the box with the key when the news comes? Now we have to go to bed. It matters not how long the day," he lifted the box by its handle, moved towards the stairs, its weight dragging the right shoulder down. "Blow out the lamp. I'll wait for you."

Painfully the slow climb of the stairs began, his shoulder dragged sideways by the mud and grass box. His breathing came in laboured catches. He leaned on the banister rail. Three times he paused, while I kept bewildered pace below, the key in my palm, weak moonlight from the window at the top of the stairs showing the hollowed wood in the centre of the steps, dark red paint on the sides, of the way.

"I want you to come to my room to show you where to find it when the news comes." He opened the door of his room that stank from the stale air and senna leaves and sweat, the moon from the river window gave light enough, but he gave me matches to light the glass lamp, and cursed as I fumbled the lighting in my fear.

"Under the wardrobe," he said, as he pushed the box between the legs of the plywood wardrobe, its brass handle shining and the silver medallions of the police caps on its top. "You'll pull it out from under the wardrobe when the news comes. You have the key?"

"But I don't want you to die."

"Now," he put his hand on my head, "I love you too, but we can't control our days, we can only pray. You have the key?"

F

The key lay in the sweat of the palm.

"You'll open the box with the key when the news comes."

The train took him to the hospital the next day but before the end of the same week it took him home again. He asked if his room was ready and immediately went there. He said he didn't want anything to eat and didn't want to be called the next morning. No one ventured near the door till Bannon climbed the stairs. When no answer greeted the timid twice-repeated knock he opened it a small way.

"You're home, Sergeant. Are you any better?"

The Sergeant was sitting up in the bed with spectacles on, going through the medical dictionary. He looked at Bannon over the spectacles but didn't answer.

"I just came up to see if there was anything I could do for you? If you wanted me to ring Neary or anything?"

At Neary's name he shouted: "No. I don't want you to do anything. I want you to get to hell down to the day-room and leave me in peace."

A scared and bewildered Bannon closed the door, came down the stairs, and there was no sound from the bedroom for several hours till suddenly a loud knocking came on the floorboards.

"He wants something." "You go up." "No, you go up." "No." It spread immediate panic.

The next knocking was loud with anger, imperative.

"Nobody'll do anything in this cursed house except me," I shouted almost in his voice.

It had been relief to see him come home, almost joy in the release: though I didn't know what to make of the shutting away in the upstairs room. The shouts at Bannon had been vicious, also I didn't know what to do with the key.

"It took you long enough to come." He was lying down in the bed, and the medical book was shut on the eiderdown to one side.

"I was in the scullery."

"You weren't all in the scullery."

"They didn't want to come," I answered and waited.

"I want something to eat."

"What would you like?"

"Anything, anything that's in the house."

"Bacon and egg or milk pudding?"

"Bacon and eggs'll do."

I held the key in my hand. I wanted to ask him what to do with the key, if he wanted it back; and my eyes kept straying under the plywood wardrobe where the bomb box must be; but the face in the bed didn't invite any questions, it warned me to get out.

That day and the next he stayed in the room, but at five o'clock the third morning he woke the whole house by clattering downstairs and even more loudly opening and closing cupboard doors and presses, muttering all the time. When we came down he'd gone out. We saw him outside examining the potato and turnip pits, the rows of winter cabbage.

After his breakfast he shaved at the old mirror and carefully combed his receding hair over the bald patches of the scalp, polished his boots, gathered the silver buttons and medallions of the tunic on the brass stick and shone them with Silvo.

On the stroke of nine he went down to the day-room. I heard his raised voice within minutes, "Nothing done right. I've told you time in and time out that these records must never be let fall behind," and the unfortunate Bannon's low excuses.

For several weeks I kept the key in my pocket, but each time I tried to ask him what I'd do with it, and if he wanted it back, I wasn't able. Eventually, one warm evening, with some anxiety, I threw it as far away towards the river as I was able, watching its flight curve between the two ash trees to fall into the sedge and wild nettles a few feet from the water.

Korea

"You saw an execution then too, didn't you?" I asked my father, and he started to tell as he rowed. He'd been captured in an ambush in late 1919, and they were shooting prisoners in Mountjoy as reprisals at that time. He thought it was he who'd be next, for after a few days they moved him to the cell next to the prison yard. He could see out through the bars. But no rap to prepare himself came to the door that night, and at daybreak he saw the two prisoners they'd decided to shoot being marched out: a man in his early thirties, and what was little more than a boy, sixteen or seventeen, and he was weeping. They blindfolded the boy, but the man refused the blindfold. When the officer shouted, the boy clicked to attention, but the man stayed as he was, chewing very slowly. He had his hands in his pockets.

"Take your hands out of your pockets," the officer shouted again, there was irritation in the voice.

The man slowly shook his head.

"It's a bit too late now in the day for that," he said.

The officer then ordered them to fire, and as the volley rang, the boy tore at his tunic over the heart, as if to pluck out the bullets, and the buttons of the tunic began to fly into the air before he pitched forward on his face.

The other heeled quietly over on his back; it must have been because of the hands in the pockets.

The officer dispatched the boy with one shot from the revolver as he lay face downward, but he pumped five bullets in rapid succession into the man, as if to pay him back for not coming to attention.

"When I was on my honeymoon years after, it was May, and we took the tram up the hill of Howth from Sutton Cross. We sat on top in the open on the wooden seats with the rail around that made it like a small ship. The sea was below, and smell of the sea and furze bloom all about, and then I looked down and saw the furze pods bursting, and the way they burst in all directions seemed shocking like the buttons when he started to tear at his tunic; I couldn't get it out of my mind all day; it destroyed the day," he said.

"It's a wonder their hands weren't tied?" I asked him as he rowed between the black navigation pan and the red where the river flowed into Oakport.

"I suppose it was because they were considered soldiers."

"Do you think the boy stood to attention because he felt that he might still get off if he obeyed the rules?"

"Sounds a bit highfalutin to me. Comes from going to school too long," he said aggressively, and I was silent. It was new to me to hear him talk about his own life at all. Before, if I asked him about the war, he'd draw fingers across his eyes as if to tear a spider web away, but it was my last summer with him on the river, and it seemed to make him want to talk, to give of himself before it ended.

Hand over hand I drew in the line that throbbed with fish; there were two miles of line, a hook on a lead line every three yards. The license allowed us a thousand hooks, but we used more. We were the last to fish this freshwater for a living.

As the eels came in over the side I cut them loose with a knife into a wire cage, where they slid over each other in their own oil, the twisted eel hook in their mouths. The other fish—pike choked on hooked perch they'd tried to swallow, bream, roach—I slid up the floorboards towards the bow of the boat. We'd sell them in the village or give them away. The hooks that hadn't been taken I cleaned and stuck in rows round the side of the wooden box. I let the line fall in its centre. After a mile he took my place in the stern and I rowed. People hadn't woken yet, and the early morning cold and mist were on the river. Outside of the slow ripple of the oars and the threshing of the fish on the line beaded with running drops of water as it came in, the river was dead silent, except for the occasional lowing of cattle on the banks.

"Have you any idea what you'll do after this summer?" he asked.

"No. I'll wait and see what comes up," I answered.

"How do you mean *what comes up*?"

"Whatever result I get in the exam. If the result is good, I'll have choices. If it's not, there won't be choices. I'll have to take what I can get."

"How good do you think they'll be?"

"I think they'll be all right, but there's no use counting chickens, is there?"

"No," he said, but there was something calculating in the face; it made me watchful of him as I rowed the last stretch of the line. The day had come, the distant noises of the farms and the first flies on the river, by the time we'd lifted the large wire cage out of the bulrushes, emptied in the morning's catch of eels, and sunk it again.

"We'll have enough for a consignment tomorrow," he said.

Each week we sent the eels live to Billingsgate in London.

"But say, say even if you do well, you wouldn't think of throwing this country up altogether and going to America?" he said, the words fumbled for as I pushed the boat, using the oar as a pole, out of the bulrushes after sinking the cage of eels, the mud rising a dirty yellow between the stems.

"Why America?"

"Well, it's the land of opportunity, isn't it, a big, expanding country; there's no room for ambition in this poky place. All there's room for is to make holes in pints of porter."

I was wary of the big words, they were not in his voice or any person's voice.

"Who'd pay the fare?" I asked.

"We'd manage that. We'd scrape it together somehow."

"Why should you scrape for me to go to America if I can get a job here?"

"I feel I'd be giving you a chance I never got. I fought for this country. And now they want to take away even the license to fish. Will you think about it anyhow?"

"I'll think about it," I answered.

Through the day he trimmed the brows of ridges in the potato field while I replaced hooks on the line and dug worms, pain of doing things for the last time as well as the boredom the knowledge brings that soon there'll be no need to do them, that they could be discarded almost now. The guilt of leaving came: I was discarding his life to assume my own, a man to row the boat would eat into the decreasing profits of the fishing, and it was even not certain he'd get renewal of his license. The tourist board had opposed the last application. They said we impoverished the coarse fishing for tourists—the tourists who came every summer from Liverpool and Birmingham in increasing numbers to sit in aluminium deck chairs on the riverbank and fish with rods. The fields we had would be a bare living without the fishing, and it'd be vinegar for him to turn what he called boarding-house zookeeper.

I saw him stretch across the wall in conversation with the cattle-dealer Farrell as I came round to put the worms where we stored them in clay in the darkness of the lavatory. Farrell leaned on the bar of his bicycle on the road. I passed into the lavatory thinking they talked about the price of cattle, but as I emptied the worms into the box, the word *Moran* came, and I carefully opened the door to listen. It was my father's voice; it was excited.

"I know. I heard the exact sum. They got ten thousand dollars when Luke was killed. Every American soldier's life is insured to the tune of ten thousand dollars."

"I heard they get two hundred and fifty dollars a month each for Michael and Sam while they're serving," he went on.

"They're buying cattle leftandright," Farrell's voice came as I closed the door and stood in the darkness, in the smell of shit and piss and the warm fleshy smell of worms crawling in too little clay.

The shock I felt was the shock I was to feel later when

I made some social blunder, the splintering of a self-esteem, and the need to crawl into some lavatory and think.

Luke Moran's body had come from Korea in a leaden casket, had crossed the stone bridge to the slow funeral bell with the big cars from the embassy behind, the coffin draped in the Stars and Stripes. Shots had been fired above the grave before they threw in the clay. There were photos of his decorations being presented to his family by a military attaché.

He'd scrape the fare, I'd be conscripted there, each month he'd get so many dollars while I served, and he'd get ten thousand if I was killed.

In the darkness of the lavatory between the boxes of crawling worms before we set the night line for the eels I knew my youth had ended.

I rowed as he let out the night line, his fingers baiting each twisted hook so beautifully that it seemed a single movement. The dark was closing from the shadow of Oakport to Nutley's boathouse, bats made ugly whirls overhead, the wings of ducks shirred as they curved down into the bay.

"Have you thought about what I said about going to America?" he asked, without lifting his eyes from the hooks and the box of worms.

"I have."

The oars dipped in the water without splash, the hole whorling wider in the calm as it slipped past him on the stern seat.

"Have you decided to take the chance then?"

"No. I'm not going."

"You won't be able to say I didn't give you the chance

when you come to nothing in this fool of a country. It'll be your own funeral."

"It'll be my own funeral," I answered, and asked after a long silence, "As you grow older, do you find your own days in the war and jails coming much back to you?"

"I do. And I don't want to talk about them. Talking about the execution disturbed me no end, those cursed buttons bursting into the air. And the most I think is that if I'd conducted my own wars, and let the fool of a country fend for itself, I'd be much better off today. And I don't want to talk about it."

I knew this silence was fixed forever as I rowed in silence till he asked, "Do you think, will it be much good to-night?"

"It's too calm," I answered.

"Unless the night wind gets up," he said anxiously.

"Unless a night wind," I repeated.

As the boat moved through the calm water and the line slipped through his fingers over the side I'd never felt so close to him before, not even when he'd carried me on his shoulders above the laughing crowd to the Final. Each move he made I watched as closely as if I too had to prepare myself to murder.

Lavin

When I knew Lavin he was close to the poorhouse but he'd still down mallet and cold chisel to limp after the young girls, crooked finger beckoning, calling, "Come, give us a peep, there must be a few little hairs beginning," and that strange inlooking smile coming over the white stubbled face while the girls, shrieking with laughter, kept backing just fast enough to stay outside his reach.

When I heard them speak of Lavin it was in puzzlement that when young and handsome he had worked such cruel hours at his trade, though he had no need because his uncle had left him Willowfield, the richest farm around, and had taken no interest in girls though he could have had his pick; and at a threshing or in a wheatfield he'd be found at nightfall gathering carelessly abandoned tools or closing gaps after the others had gone drinking or to dress for the dances. Neither could they understand his sudden heavy drinking in Billy Burns's: if before he had to enter a pub he'd accept nothing but lemonade. Burns was blamed for giving him credit when his money ran out; and after he seized and held in the house the gipsy girl who sold him paper flowers with wire stems, it was the same Burns who gave him the money to buy the gipsies off in return for Willowfield. The gipsies had told him that if he didn't pay what they wanted they'd come and cut him with rusted iron. What money he was able to earn afterwards was from his trade, and that steadily dwindled as machinery replaced the horse. All of his roof had fallen in except the kitchen, where oats and green weeds grew out of the thatch. Whatever work he had he did outside on the long hacked bench except when it was too cold or wet. The first time I stopped to watch him it was because of the attraction of what's forbidden. He was shaping a section of a cart wheel but put down mallet and chisel to say, that strange smile I'll always remember coming over his face, "Those sisters of yours are growing into fine sprigs. Have you looked to see if any of them have started a little thatch?"

"No," his smile frightened me.

"It should be soft, light, a shading," his voice lingered on the words, I felt his eyes did not see past their smiling.

"I haven't seen," I said and started to watch the roads for anybody coming.

"You should keep your eyes skinned then. All you have to do is to keep your eyes skinned, man," the voice was harder.

"I don't sleep in their rooms."

"No need to sleep in the same room, man. Just keep your eyes skinned. Wait till you hear them go to the pot and walk in by mistake. It'll be cocked enough to see if it has started to thatch," the voice had grown rhythmical and hard.

It was more desire to see into this hot dark I glimpsed behind the smile than his constant pestering for the information made me begin to watch.

"The two eldest have hair but the others haven't," I told him.

"The others have just a bald ridge with the slit," he pursued fiercely.

"Yes." I'd have escaped but he seized me by the lapels.

"The hair is fairer than on their heads?"

"Yes."

"Fair and soft? A shade?"

"Yes, but let me go."

"Soft and fair. The young ivy covering the slit," he let me go as the voice grew caressing and the smile flooded over the face.

"So fair you can see the skin through it yet. A shading," he gloated and then, "Will you come with me a minute inside?"

"I have to go."

He turned as if I no longer was there and limped, the boot tongueless and unlaced, to the door, and though I hurried frightened away I heard the bolt scrape shut before I was out of earshot.

I avoided Lavin all that winter, I'd heard his foot was worse though and that he was unlikely to see another winter outside the poorhouse, it should have assuaged my fear but it did not, and besides I'd fallen in love with Charley Casey.

Charley Casey was dull in school; but he was good at games, and popular, with a confident laugh and white teeth and blue dark hair: he had two dark-haired sisters of seventeen and nineteen, who were both beautiful, and a young widowed mother, and there hung about him that glamour of a house of ripe women. I helped him at his exercises, and in return he partnered me in handball. We started to skate in the evenings together on the shallow pond and to go to the river when the days grew warmer. I was often sick with anxiety, days he was absent—able to concentrate on nothing but the bell that would set me free to race to his house to see what had kept him away.

I tried to get him to read *David Copperfield* at that time so that we could share its world but he had always excuses. When the school closed and I had to go with my family to the sea he promised the day I left that he'd have it read by the time I got back: and instead of playing or swimming that week I spent most time alone among the sandhills imagining the conversations about *David Copperfield* on the riverbank in so many days when the slow week at the sea would be over.

"I read a good deal of it," he answered to my first impatient question. The morning we got back I'd rushed to his house without waiting to eat, but as I pursued him with questions it grew depressingly clear that he'd not read a word and he admitted, "I did my best to read it but I fell asleep. It's too hot to read. I'll read it when it rains."

"You promised," I accused bitterly; it broke me he could fall asleep over the beloved book.

"Honest, I'll read it when it rains. Why can't we go to the river same as before!"

"I don't want to go to the river. Why don't we go to see Lavin?" I said in thirst for some perversity or desire to degrade.

"That's a great idea," I was taken aback by his enthusiasm. "Why don't we see old John?"

I walked slowly and sullenly to Lavin's, resentful that he had fallen so easily in with my proposal.

Tools beginning to rust were outside on the old bench

and the door was open. Lavin sat inside, his foot upon a footrest. The foot was wrapped in multicoloured rags that included red flannel and stank in the heat. Casey crossed the shaving-littered floor to go up to where Lavin sat at the empty fireplace to ask gaily, "How's the old foot, John?"

"Playing me up, Charley Boy, but Himself was never in better order."

"I've no doubt," Charley laughed loudly.

I stood close to the door in smouldering anger and outrage.

"How are the two beauties of sisters? The thatch must be good and black and thick, eh? Brimmin' with juice inside, or have they shaved?" The smile came instantly, the repetitious fondling voice.

"No. They didn't shave it, John. It's as thick as thatch. Not that thatch is going to be all that thick above your head for long," Casey laughed.

"Never mind the roof now. How is little John Charles coming along? Sprouting nicely?" he touched Casey's fly gently with his fingertips.

"You have to show me yours first. You never saw such a weapon as old John has," Casey laughed and winked towards me at the door.

"No sooner said than done," Lavin at once opened his trousers, what he took out looked to me enormous and brutal, it was stiff.

"A fair weapon and as stiff as a stake," Casey gripped it in his fist.

"Know the only place the stiffs get in: the cunt and the grave," Lavin joked and I noticed his mouth full of the black stumps of teeth as he laughed.

"I bet you put it stiff and hard into the gipsy, old Johnny Balls," Casey teased.

"Yeah, and what about seeing little John Charles now?"

"Fire ahead," Casey laughed and I wanted to shout but wasn't able as Lavin unbuttoned Casey's fly and gently started to play with it in his fingers.

"Sprouting along royal, fit for milking any day."

He fondled it until it was erect and then stretched to take a heavy carpenter's rule from the mantel.

"An increase of a good inch since the last time upon my soul," he said. "Why don't you come up from the door to see which little John Charles is farthest advanced?"

"No," I had to fight back tears of rage and humiliation,

"Come on," Casey said challengingly. "Let old John compare them."

"I don't want."

"Have it your own way so," he said, and as he took the rule to measure Lavin I left and waited in a fury outside. Either he grew scared alone or had enough because he soon followed.

"Why did you do it?" I attacked immediately he came.

"Oh, I like to take a hand at old John every now and then and get him all worked up," he said casually.

"What did you let him fool around with you for?"

"What does it matter? It gets him all worked up."

"I think it's disgusting," I said with puritanical bitterness disturbed by feelings that had never touched me so fiercely before.

"Oh, what does it matter? He'll soon be in the poorhouse. Why don't we go for a swim?"

I walked in sullen silence by his side across the bridge. I

G

wanted to swim with him, but I wanted to reject him, and in my heart I hated him. I calmed as we walked and at the boathouse helped him lift someone's night line, it had no fish though the hooks had been cleaned of bait. We started to talk again as we went to where the high whitethorns shielded the river from the road. We stripped on the bank and swam and afterwards lay on the warm moss watching the bream shoal out beyond the reeds, their black fins moving sluggish above the calm surface, white gleam of the bellies as they slowly rolled, until harness bells sounded on the road behind the whitethorns, and at the iron gate where the whitethorns ended two gipsy caravans and a spring cart came into our view. The little round curtained window in the back glittered in the sun, and two dogs roped to the axle trotted head low mechanically between the red wheels. Now and then a whip cracked above the horses' head into the jingling of the harness bells.

"Do you think Lavin did what he was supposed to do to the gipsy girl?" I asked.

"He'd hardly have to pay with the farm if he didn't," Casey answered with quiet logic. The image of the monstrous penis being driven deep in the guts of the struggling gipsy girl made me shiver with excitement on the moss.

"It'd be good if we had two caravans, you and me, like the caravans gone past. You and me would live in one caravan. We'd keep four women in the other. We'd ride around Ireland. We'd make them do anything we'd want to," if Casey had been more forward with Lavin I was leading now.

"It'd be great," he answered.

"They'd strip the minute we said strip. If they didn't

we'd whip them. We'd whip them with those whips that have bits of metal on the ends. We'd whip them until the blood came and they'd to put arms round our knees for mercy."

"Yes. We'd make them get down on their hands and knees naked and do them from behind the way the bull does," Casey said and dived sideways to seize a frog in the grass, he took a dried stem of reed and began to insert it in the frog, "That's what'll tickle him, I'm telling you."

"Why couldn't we do it together?" I tentatively asked stiff with excitement, and he understood without me having to say more.

"I'll do it to you first," he said, the dead reed sticking out of the frog in his hand, "and then you'll do it to me."

"Why don't you let me do it to you first and then you can have as long as you like on me?"

"No."

The fear was unspoken: whoever took his pleasure first would have the other in his power and then might not surrender his own body. We avoided each other's eyes. I watched the dead reed being moved in and out of the frog.

"They say it hurts," I said and there was the relief of the escape now from having to go through with it.

"It'd probably hurt too much," Charley Casey was eager to agree. "It'd be better to get two women and hurt them. They say a frog can only live so long under water."

"Why don't we see?"

I found a stone along the bank and we tied one of the frog's legs with fishing line to the stone. We took it some hundred yards up the bank to where a shallow stream joined the river. We dropped the stone and watched the frog claw upwards but each time dragged back by the line, until it weakened, and it drowned.

We went silent across the Bridge, already changing. I helped him at school for sometime afterward but in the evenings we avoided each other, as if we vaguely glimpsed some shameful truth we were afraid to come to know together.

I never saw Lavin again, they took him to the poorhouse that October when the low hedges were blue with sloes, though by then the authorities, in their kindness, referred to it as the Resthome for Senior Citizens.

Casey is now married with children and runs a pub called the *Crown and Anchor* somewhere in Manchester but I've never had any wish to look him up, he seldom in fact enters my mind: but as I grow older hardly a day passes but this picture of Lavin comes to trouble me, it is of him when he was young, and they said handsome, gathering the scattered tools at nightfall in a clean wheatfield after the others had gone drinking or to change for the dances.

My Love, My Umbrella

It was the rain, the constant weather of this city, made my love inseparable from the umbrella, a black umbrella, white stitching on the seams of the imitation leather over the handle, the metal point bent where it was caught in Mooney's grating as we raced for the last bus to the garage out of Abbey Street. The band was playing when we met, the Blanchardstown Fife and Drum. They were playing *Some day he'll come along/ The man I love/And he'll be big and strong/ The man I love* at the back of the public lavatory on Burgh Quay, facing a few persons on the pavement in front of the Scotch House. It was the afternoon of a Sunday.

"It is strange, the band," I said; her face flinched away, and in the same movement back, turned to see who'd spoken. Her skin under the black hair had the glow of health and youth, and the solidity at the bones of the hips gave promise of a rich seedbed.

"It's strange," she answered, and I was at once anxious for her body.

The conductor stood on a wooden box, continually breaking off his conducting to engage in some running argument with a small grey man by his side, but whether he waved his stick jerkedly or was bent in argument seemed to make no difference to the players. They turned their pages. The music plodded on, *Some day he'll come along/ The man I love/And he'll be big and strong/ The man I love*. At every interval they looked towards the clock, Mooney's clock across the river.

"They're watching the clock," I said.

"Why?" her face turned again.

"They'll only play till the opening hour."

I too anxiously watched the clock. I was afraid she'd go when the band stopped. Lights came on inside the Scotch House. The music hurried. A white-aproned barman, a jangle of keys into the quickened music, began to unlock the folding shutters and with a resounding clash drew them back. As the tune ended the conductor signalled to the band that they could put away their instruments, got down from his box, and started to tap the small grey man on the shoulder with the baton as he began to argue in earnest. The band came across the road towards the lighted globes inside the Scotch House, where already many of their audience waited impatiently on the slow pulling of the pints. The small grey man carried the conductor's box as they passed together in.

"It is what we said would happen."

"Yes."

The small family cars were making their careful way home across the bridge after their Sunday outings to their cold ham and tomato and lettuce, the wind blowing from the mouth of the river, gulls screeching above the stink of its low tide, as I forced the inanities towards an invitation.

"Would you come with me for a drink?"

"Why?" She blushed as she looked me full in the face.

"Why not?"

"I said I'd be back for tea."

"We can have sandwiches."

"But why do you want me to?"

"I'd like very much if you come. Will you come?"

"All right I'll come but I don't know why."

It was how we began, the wind blowing from the mouth of the river while the Blanchardstown Fife and Drum downed their first thirstquencher in the Scotch House.

They'd nothing but beef left in Mooney's after the weekend. We had stout with our beef sandwiches. Soon, in the drowsiness of the stout, we did little but watch the others drinking. I pointed out a poet to her, I recognized him from his pictures in the paper. His shirt was open-necked inside a gaberdine coat and he wore a hat with a small feather in its band. She asked me if I liked poetry.

"When I was younger," I said. "Do you?"

"Not very much."

She asked me if I could hear what the poet was saying to the four men at his table who continually plied him with whiskey. I hadn't heard. Now we both listened. He was saying he loved the blossoms of Kerr Pinks more than roses, a man could only love what he knew well, and it was the quality of the love mattered and not the accident. The whole table said they'd drink to that, but he glared at them as if slighted, and as if to avoid the glare they called for a round of doubles. While the drinks were coming from the bar the poet turned aside and took a canister from his pocket. The inside of the lid was coated with a white powder which he quickly licked clean. She thought it was baking soda, her father in the country took baking soda for his stomach. We had more stout and we noticed, while each new round was coming, the poet turned away from the table to lick clean the fresh coat of soda on the inside of the canister lid.

That was the way our first evening went. People who came into the pub were dripping with rain and we stayed until they'd draped the towels over the pump handles and called "Time" in the hope the weather would clear, but it did not.

The beat of rain was so fierce when we came out that the street was a dance of glass shapes, and they reminded me of the shape of the circle of blackened spikes on the brass candleshrine which hold the penny candles before the altar.

"Does it remind you of the candlespikes?" I asked.

"Yes, now that you mention it."

Perhaps the rain, the rain will wash away the poorness of our attempts at speech, our bodies will draw closer, closer than our speech, I hoped, as she returned on the throat my kiss in the bus, and that we'd draw closer to a meal of each other's flesh; and from the bus, under the beat of rain on the umbrella, we walked beyond Fairview church.

"Will I be able to come in?" I asked.

"It would cause trouble."

"You have your own room?"

"The man who owns the house watches. He would make trouble."

Behind the church was a dead end overhung with old trees, and the street lights did not reach far as the wall at its end, a grey orchard wall with some ivy.

"Can we stay here a short time then?"

I hung upon the silence, afraid she'd use the rain as

excuse, and breathed when she said, "Not for long, it is late."

We moved under the umbrella out of the street light, fumbling for certain footing between the tree roots.

"Will you hold the umbrella?"

She took the imitation leather with the white stitching in her hands.

Our lips moved on the saliva of our mouths as I slowly undid the coat button. I tried to control the trembling so as not to tear the small white buttons of the blouse. Coat, blouse, brassière as names of places on a road. I globed the warm soft breasts in hands. I leaned across the cold metal above the imitation leather she held in her hands to take the small nipples gently in teeth, the steady beat on the umbrella broken by irregular splashes from the branches.

Will she let me? I was afraid as I lifted the woollen skirt; and slowly I moved hands up the soft insides of the thighs, and instead of the "No" I feared and waited for, the handle became a hard pressure as she pressed on my lips.

I could no longer control the trembling as I felt the sheen of the knickers, I drew them down to her knees, and parted the lips to touch the juices. She hung on my lips. She twitched as the fingers went deeper. She was a virgin.

A memory of the cow pumping on the rubbered arm of the inseminator as the thick juice falls free and he injects the semen with the glass plunger came with a desire to hurt. "It hurts," the cold metal touched my face, the rain duller on the sodden cloth by now.

"I won't hurt you," I said, and pumped low between her thighs, lifting high the coat and skirts so that the seed fell free into the mud and rain, and after resting on each other's mouth I replaced the clothes.

Under the umbrella, one foot asleep, we walked past the small iron railings of the gardens towards her room, and at the gate I left her with, "Where will we meet again?"

We would meet at eight against the radiators inside the Metropole.

We met against those silver radiators three evenings every week for long. We went to cinemas or sat in pubs, it was the course of our love, and as it always rained we made love under the umbrella beneath the same trees in the same way. They say the continuance of sexuality is due to the penis having no memory, and mine each evening spilt its seed into the mud and decomposing leaves as if it was always for the first time.

Sometimes we told each other stories.

The story she told that most interested me had some cruelty, which is possibly why I found it exciting.

She'd grown up on a small farm. The neighbouring farm was owned by a Pat Moran who lived on it alone after the death of his mother. As a child she used to look for nests of hens that were laying wild on his farm and he used to bring her chocolates or oranges from the fairs. As she grew, feeling the power of her body, she began to provoke him, until one evening on her way to the well through his fields, where he was pruning a whitethorn hedge with a billhook, she lay in the soft grass and showed him so much of her body beneath the clothes that he dropped the billhook and seized her. She struggled loose and shouted as she ran, "I'll tell my Daddy, you pig." She was far too afraid to tell her father, but it was as if a wall came down between her and

Pat Moran who soon afterwards sold his farm and went to England though he'd never known any other life but that of a small farmer.

She'd grown excited in the telling and asked me what I thought of the story. I said that I thought life was often that way. She then, her face flushed, asked me if I had any stories in my life. I said I did, but there was a story that I read in the evening paper that had interested me, since it had indirectly got to do with us.

It had been a report of a prosecution. In the rush hour at Bank station in London two city gents had lost tempers in the queue and had assaulted each other with umbrellas. They had inflicted severe injuries with the umbrellas. The question before the judge: was it a case of common assault or, much more seriously, assault with dangerous weapon with intent to wound? In view of the extent of the injuries inflicted it had not been an easy decision, but he eventually found for common assault, since he didn't want the thousands of peaceable citizens who used their umbrellas properly to feel that when they travelled to and from work they were carrying dangerous weapons. He fined and bound both gentlemen to the peace, warned them severely as to their future conduct, but he did not impose a prison sentence, as he'd be forced to do if he'd found the umbrella to be a dangerous weapon.

"What do you think of the story?"

"I think it's pretty silly. Let's go home," she said though it was an hour from the closing hour, raising the umbrella as soon as we reached the street. It was raining as usual.

"Why did you tell that silly story about the umbrellas?" she asked on the bus.

"Why did you tell the story of the farmer?"

"They were different," she said.

"Yes. They were different," I agreed. For some reason she resented the story.

In the rain we made love again, she the more fierce, and after the seed had spilled she said, "Wait," and moving on a dying penis, under the unsteady umbrella in her hands, she trembled towards an inarticulate cry of pleasure, and as we walked into the street lamp I asked, we had so fallen into the habit of each other, "Would you think we should ever get married?" "Kiss me," she leaned across the steel between us. "Do you think we ever should?" I repeated. "What would it mean to you?" she asked.

What I had were longings or fears rather than any meanings. To go with her on the train to Thurles on a Friday evening in summer, and walk the three miles to her house from the station. To be woken the next morning by the sheepdog barking the postman to the door and have tea and brown bread and butter in a kitchen with the cool of brown flagstones and full of the smell of recent baking.

Or fear of a housing estate in Clontarf, escape to the Yacht Sunday mornings to read the papers in peace over pints, come home dazed in the midday light of the sea front with a peace offering of sweets to the Sunday roast. Afterwards in the drowse of food and drink to be woken by, "You promised to take us out for the day, Daddy," until you backed the hire-purchased Volkswagen out the gateway and drove to Howth and stared out at the sea through the gathering condensation on the semicircles the wipers made on the windshield, and quelled quarrels and cries of the bored children in the back seat.

I decided not to tell her either of these pictures as they might seem foolish to her.

"We'd have to save if we were to think about it," I heard her voice.

"We don't save very much, do we?"

"At the rate the money goes in the pubs we might as well throw our hat at it. Why did you ask?"

"Because", it was not easy to answer then, when I had to think, "I like being with you."

"Why, why," she asked, "did you tell that stupid story about the umbrellas?"

"It happened, didn't it? And we never make love without an umbrella. It reminded me of your body."

"Such rubbish," she said angrily. "The sea and sand and hot beach at night, needing only a single sheet, that'd make some sense, but an umbrella?"

It was the approach of summer and it was the false confidence it brings that undid me. It rained less. A bright moonlit night I asked her to hold the umbrella.

"For what?"

She was so fierce that I pretended it'd been a joke.

"I don't see much of a joke standing like a fool holding an umbrella to the blessed moonlight," she said and we made love awkwardly, the umbrella lying in the dry leaves; but I was angry that she wouldn't fall in with my wish, and another night when she asked, "Where are you going on your holidays?" I lied that I didn't know. "I'll go home if I haven't enough money. And you?" I asked. She didn't answer. I saw she resented that I'd made no effort to include her in the holiday. "Sun and sand and sea," I thought maliciously and decided to break free from her.

Summer was coming, and the world full of possibilities. I would be tied to no stake. I did not lead her under the trees behind the church, but left after kissing her lightly, "Good night." Instead of arranging to meet as usual at the radiators I said, "I'll ring you during the week." Her look of anger and hatred elated me. "Ring if you want," she said as she angrily closed the door.

I was so clownishly elated that I threw the umbrella high in the air and laughing loudly caught it coming down, and there was the exhilaration of staying free those first days, but it soon palled. In the empty room trying to read, while the trains went by at the end of the garden with its two apple trees and one pear, I began to realize I'd fallen more into the habit of her than I'd known. Not wanting to have to see the umbrella I put it behind the wardrobe, but it seemed to be more present than ever there; and often the longing for her lips, her body, grew close to sickness, and eventually dragged me to the telephone, though I wouldn't admit it was any weakness, it was no more than a whim.

"I didn't expect to hear from you after this time," were her first words.

"I was ill."

She was ominously silent as if she knew it for the lie that it was.

"I wondered if we could meet?"

"If you want," she answered. "When?"

"What about tonight?"

"I cannot but tomorrow night is all right."

"At eight then at the radiators?"

"Say at Wynn's Hotel instead."

The imagination, quickened by distance and uncertainty,

found it hard to wait till the seven of the next day, but when the bus drew in at seven, and she was already waiting, the mind slopped back to its original complacency.

"Where'd you like to go?"

"Some place quiet. Where we can talk," she said.

Crossing the bridge and past where the band had played the first day we met, the Liffey was still in the summer evening.

"I missed you a great deal," I tried to draw close, her hands were white gloved.

"What was your sickness?"

"Some kind of flu."

She was hard and separate as she walked. It was one of the new lounge bars she picked as quiet, with piped music and red cushions. The bar was empty, the barman polishing glasses. He brought the guinness and sweet sherry to the table.

"What did you want to say?" I asked when the barman had returned to polishing the glasses.

"That I've thought about it and that our going out is a waste of time. It's a waste of your time and mine."

It was as if a bandage had been torn from an open wound.

"But why?"

"It will come to nothing."

"You've got someone else then?"

"That's got nothing to do with it."

"But why then?"

"I don't love you."

"But we've had many happy evenings together."

"Yes, but it's not enough."

"I thought that after a time we would get married," I would grovel on the earth or anything to keep her then. Little by little my life had fallen into her keeping, it was only in the loss I had come to know it, life without her the pain of the loss of my own life without the oblivion the dead have, all longing changed to die out of my own life on her lips, on her thighs, since it was only in her it lived.

"It wouldn't work," she said and sure of her power, "All those wasted evenings under that old umbrella. And that moonlit night you tried to get me to hold it up like some eejit. What did you take me for?"

"I meant no harm and couldn't we try to make a new start?"

"No. There should be something magical about getting married and we know too much about each other. There's nothing more to discover."

"You mean with our bodies?"

"Yes."

She moved to go and I was desperate.

"Will you have one more drink?"

"No, I don't really want."

"Can we not meet just once more?"

"No," she rose to go. "It'd only uselessly prolong it and come to the same thing in the end."

"Are you so sure? If there was just one more chance?"

"No. And there's no need for you to see me to the bus. You can finish your drink."

"I don't want," and followed her through the swing door.

At the stop in front of the Bank of Ireland I tried one last time, "Can I not see you home this last night?"

"No, it's easier this way."

"You're meeting someone else then?"

"No. And it's beside the point."

It was clean as a knife. I watched her climb on the bus, fumble in her handbag, take the fare from a small purse, open her hand to the conductor as the bus turned the corner. I watched to see if she'd look back, if she'd give any sign, but she did not; all my love and life had gone and I had to wait till it was gone to know it.

I then realized I'd left the umbrella in the pub, and started to return slowly for it. I went through the swing door, took the umbrella from where it leaned against the red cushion, raised it and said, "Just left this behind," to the barman's silent inquiry, as if the performance of each small act would numb the pain.

I got to no southern sea or city that summer. The body I'd tried to escape from became my only thought. In the late evening after pub-close, I'd stop in terror at the thought of what hands were fondling her body, and would if I had power have made all casual sex a capital offence. On the street I'd see a coat or dress she used to wear, especially a cheap blue dress with white dots, zipped at the back, that was fashionable that summer, and with beating heart would push through the crowds till I was level with the face that wore the dress but the face was never her face.

I often rang her, pleading, and she consented to see me for one lunch hour when I said I was desperate. We walked aimlessly through streets of the lunch hour, and I'd to hold back tears as I thanked her for her kindness, though when she'd given me all her evenings and body I'd hardly noticed. The same night after pub-close I went—driven by

H

the urge that brings people back to the rooms where they once lived and no longer live, or to sleep in the same sheets and bed of their close dead the night after they're taken from the house—and stood out of the street lamps under the trees where so often we had stood, in the hope that some meaning of my life or love would come, but only the night hardened about the growing absurdity of a man standing under an umbrella beneath the drip from the green leaves of the trees.

Through my love it was the experience of my own future death I was passing through, for the life of the desperate equals the anxiety of death, and before time had replaced all its bandages I found relief in movement, in getting on buses and riding to the terminus; and one day at Killester I heard the conductor say to the driver as they sat downstairs through their ten-minute rest, "Jasus this country is going to the dogs entirely. There's a gent up there who looks normal enough who must umpteen times this last year have come out here to nowhere and back," and as I listened I felt as a patient after a long illness when the doctor says, "You can start getting up tomorrow," and I gripped the black umbrella with an almost fierce determination to be as I was before, unknowingly happy under the trees, and the umbrella, in the wet evenings that are the normal weather of this city.

Peaches

The shark stank far as the house, above it the screech of the sea birds; it'd stink until the birds had picked the bones clean, when the skeleton would begin to break up in the sun. The man reluctantly closed the door and went back to making coffee. He liked to stare out the door to the sea over coffee in the mornings. When he'd made the coffee he put the pot with bread and honey and a bowl of fruit on the table in the centre of the red-tiled floor. The windows on the sea were shuttered, light coming from the two windows on the mountain at the back and a small side window on the empty concrete pool without. He was about to say the breakfast was ready when he saw the woman examining the scar under her eye in the small silver-framed mirror. Her whole body stiffened with intensity as she examined it. He cursed under his breath and waited.

"It makes me look forty," he heard the slow sobs. He lifted and replaced a spoon but knew it was useless to say anything.

"If we get the divorce I'll sue you for this," she said with uncontrolled ferocity in a heavy foreign accent. She was small but beautifully proportioned with straight wheaten hair that hung to her shoulders.

"It wasn't all my fault," he lifted the spoon again.

"You were drunk."

"I had four cervezas."

"You were drunk. As you're always drunk except some hours in the mornings."

"If you hadn't loosened that rope to put in the cheese it wouldn't have happened."

He'd bought a fifteen-litre jar of red wine in Vera, it was cheaper there than in the local shops, and had roped it in the wooden box behind the Vespa. When he was drinking at the bar she'd loosened the rope to put some extra cheese and crystalized almonds in the box. He hadn't noticed the rope loose round the wickerwork of the jar when leaving. The loose rope made no difference on the tar but the last mile was a rutted dirt track. The Vespa had to be ridden on the shoulders of the road not much wider than the width of the wheels. Drowsy with the beer and the fierce heat he drove automatically until he found the wheels losing their grip in the dust on the edge of the shoulder. When he went to pull it out to the firm centre of the shoulder the fifteen litres started to swing loose in its rope at the back, swinging the wheels farther into the loose dust.

There was all the time in the world to switch off the engine so that the wheels wouldn't spin and to tell her to hold his body once he knew he was about to crash, and he remembered the happiness of the certainty that nothing he could do would avert the crash. Shielded by his body she would have been unhurt but her face came across his shoulder to strike the driving-mirror. Above him on the road she'd cried out at the blood on his face but it was her own blood flowing from the mirror's gash below her eye.

"I'm ugly, ugly, ugly," she now cried.

"The doctor said the scar'd heal and it doesn't make you ugly."

"You want to kill me. Once it was Iris." She ignored what he'd said and started to examine two thin barely visible scars down her cheek in the mirror. "She tore me with her nails when she wanted to kill me. Both of you want to kill me."

"All children fight."

"Jesus," she swore. "You even want to take her side. You want to pretend that nothing happened. Jesus, Jesus."

"No," the man raised his voice, angry now. "I know all children fight. That they're all animals. And I do know I didn't want to kill you."

"Everything I say or do you criticize. Always you take the others' side," she was again close to crying.

"Earlier it starts in the morning and earlier," he said about the fighting.

"Who was its cause? If we ever get a divorce . . ."

"O, Jesus Christ," the man broke in, he clasped his head between his hands, and then steps sounded on the hard red sandstone that led from the house to the dirt-track. The woman at once moved out of sight to a part of the L-shape of the room where the cooker was, whispering fiercely, "Don't open the door yet," and began quickly drying her face, powdering, drawing the brush frantically through her wheaten hair. He made a noise with the chair to let who-ever was outside know he was coming as she whispered, "Not yet. Do I look all right?"

"You look fine."

The man moved with exaggerated slowness to the door.

Outside in the sun hat and flowered shirt and shorts stood Mr. McGregor with an empty biscuit tin and a bunch of yellow roses.

"I thought your wife might like these," he proffered the yellow roses, "and that you might find this useful for bread or something," in a Canadian drawl.

He was their nearest neighbour, a retired timber millionaire who'd built the red villa with its private beach a few hundred metres up the road for his retirement, and now lived with his two servants and roses there. Even his children wouldn't come to him on visits because of his miserliness, which was legendary. He got round the villages in a battered red Renault but once a month the grey Rolls was taken out of the garage for him to drive to the bank in Murcia. Money and roses seemed his only passions, and often in loneliness he came to them with roses and something like this empty biscuit tin which otherwise he'd have to throw away.

"Would you like to have some coffee?" the man asked when his wife had accepted the roses.

Over the tepid coffee they listened for an hour to the state of roses, the cost of water, and the precariousness of the world's monetary system.

When he'd gone they examined the empty biscuit box: Huntley and Palmer Figrolls it had once held, and suddenly they both started to laugh at once. The woman came into the man's arms and lifted her mouth to be kissed.

"We won't fight, will we?"

"I don't want to fight."

"Don't worry about the eyes. We'll never have the divorce?"

"Never."

She started to clear the dishes from the table, humming happily as she did. "It's bad to fight. It's good to be brisk. Do you know who loves you?"

He said, "I think you're very beautiful," glad of a respite he knew wouldn't last for long.

II

"Why did we come here to this shocking country in the first place?" the woman accused.

"It was cheap and there was sea and sun and we thought it would be a good place to work," he enumerated defensively.

"And you know how much work has been done?"

"Yes. None."

"We could have stayed in hotels as cheaply as it costs to rent here. Neither of us wanted to leave Barcelona when we did. But because those phoney painter bastards had to have a taxi because of their baby you came when you did. They wanted you to come to get you to pay half of their taxi fare. When we could have travelled slowly and cheaply we had that terrible fourteen-hour drive with the baby slobbering and crying."

He remembered the scent of orange blossom coming in the open window, small dark shapes of the orange trees outside the path of the headlights and Norman, the painter, saying in a voice as if all his poetical glands were exuding juices, "Smell the orange blossom, sweetie, isn't it marvellous, isn't it marvellous to be here in Spain?" and then turning to yell into the dark back of the taxi, "For Christ's sake, sweetie, can't you get him to shut up for one minute."

"Yes. It was horrible but we were dependent on them for the language and our way about here," the man said.

"*We would have managed*," the woman enunciated each word separately, in slow derision.

"They put us up after the crash," the man said.

"Yes, even you insisted on leaving before you were able to walk, with him strutting naked round our beds with an erection, going on about the marvels of nudity and bringing those awful paintings up for us to see when we had no choice but to look at them."

"We've finished with those people."

"Yes, but they'd to practically shit all over you before you did anything."

They'd come with their child from the village to swim at the sea for the day and Norman had behaved as if in his own house; he'd gone upstairs after swimming and started to shower without asking. The man had asked them to leave then, it had been the last straw in a long series of irritations.

"They'd practically to shit all over the house before you asked them to leave," the woman taunted.

"Can't you shut up and give me some peace?"

"And now we can't even open doors or windows because of the shark. I don't know what brought us to this country. Why did I ever leave my own nice birches?" She started to cry.

"Can't you, can't you shut up!" the man said.

"And you're not going to provoke me into hitting you. It's too easy that way."

An image of blood streaming down her finger from the

splinters of a wine glass he'd swept once from her hand came, the look of triumph on her face as she said, "Now we see the street angel in his royal colours—nothing but a mean, mean bully."

"You're going to have to accept the fact of your own hatred of me. There's no use temporarily absolving it by provoking me to violence."

"Bah," she said, "I laugh at that. I wouldn't even bother to answer that."

III

The man swept the dead spiders and scorpions and lizards across the floor of the empty pool and shovelled them out on to the bank. The dry scorpions broke into their sections, but the spiders and lizards lay stiff as in their life on the bank of old mortar and gravel.

The clean floor of the pool was ready for the waterman when he came. He backed up his small tanker, originally designed to carry petrol or fuel oil, to the edge of the pool. He'd saved the money to buy the tanker by working for one year in a steel works in Düsseldorf. He connected the ragged pipe to the end of the tanker, and when he turned the brass handle the water started to run into the pool with several small jets leaking out on the way. The woman came out in a blue bathrobe trimmed with white on the edges, and the three started to watch in the simple fascination of water filling the empty pool.

"The fish, the fish it stinks," the man pointed to the shore.

"Yes, it stinks," the man answered.

"What did you think of Germany?"

"The roads, great roads, much speed."

Then he suddenly stiffened, gave a sharp cry of fear, and seized the shovel by the side of the pool, pointing to a scorpion, still, between two stones close to the wall of the house. In a panic he started to beat at the scorpion with the shovel until he made paste of it against the bone-hard ground. When he'd put the shovel aside he caught his ankle in his hand, miming gestures of pain.

"Bad, bad," he said. "I've seen men made babies by the stings."

"It's from the spiders," the woman said. "It's the only thing outside the humans that commits suicide."

It was a favourite subject of hers, the parallels between animal and human behaviour; it bored him; but mention of suicide brought him suddenly back the early days of their relationship in that country of snow and birch trees and white houses rising out of red granite against a frozen sea, a light of metal that made the oranges and lemons shine as lamps in the harbour market. It was before they married, he was waiting for his papers to come, and they were living in one of the houses along the shore, minutes away from the middle of the city.

"It's owned by the Actors Union for the actors when they get too old to act," she'd explained to him.

"But how does it come that you who are young and successful can get a room here?"

"There's not enough old ones. They have empty places."

"But where are the old then?"

"They've gone to the seaside."

He at once accepted that the Actors Union had two houses, and the old had a choice of a house in the city or a house by the seaside—until an evening over brandies and coffee with a friend of hers, the quiet Anselm, who was more interested in the history of rocking chairs than in his legal practice, he had remarked, "It is extraordinary that the Actors Union give the retired a choice of a house in the city or by the sea."

"Why?"

"She said that the reason she had a room in the old actors' house was that there were vacant rooms because some of the retired preferred to live in another house at the seaside, that they had choice."

"No, no," she'd overheard from the kitchen where she was talking with Anselm's wife. "No, no. I meant that they'd gone to the suicide."

Suddenly he grew aware of her hostile stare at the pool's edge. Perhaps he was neglecting the waterman, he quickly asked him if he'd have something to drink. He wanted water. When they'd given him the drink and paid him, the waterman told them he'd to hurry as he'd to bring two loads of water for the Canadian's roses before lunch.

IV

As soon as the tanker moved towards the dirt-track the man started to pump the water up to the tank on the roof, though he knew the woman was staring at his back with arms folded. The wooden handle of the pump had split, was held together with a rope, and was loose and awkward about the iron spike.

"I want to speak to you about something," her voice was cold.

"What?" he stopped.

"When I was talking to the waterman you never listened to one word."

"I did."

"What?"

"About the scorpion."

"Anybody'd see you were miles away but you want to be listened to yourself. And you start to pump to avoid having to listen to anything."

"I want to get the water up."

"Be honest. You're either pumping water up. Or oiling the floor. Or walking on the beach. Or drunk in the rocking chair staring at the sea. Or running to the village for one thing or another."

"Someone has to get the things."

"Not that much. The child doesn't always have to be running messages for Mammy," her voice mimicked the singsong of a child's voice.

"Can't you shut up?"

"And you've done no work for more than a year now. Except run messages for Mammy," she continued the mimicry.

"So I haven't done any work. Well, I haven't. And I want to pump the water up."

"That's what you're running from—your work and from me. I am married to a man who can neither talk nor work."

"You have to wait for work to come. Why don't you do the work if you're so keen on it then?"

"I've done the translations for the theatre."

He was about to say in irritation that translation wasn't

work but drew it back, there'd be enough quarrelling for one morning.

"I want to pump the water up," he said.

"All right pump the water up," she said and went in. As he pumped the water up, both hands on the loose rope, he heard the sharp precise taps of her typewriter through the creak of the pump and the water falling in the tank from the upstairs room.

When the tank was full, the overflow spilling down on the crushed scorpion, he went towards the fig trees in the hollow between the house and mountain. He sat under the trees to save pumping up the water. He picked a place between the blackened and dried turds under the trees. When his own smell started to rise above the shark smell and the encircling flies, he heard the typewriter stop and when he was close to the house the lavatory upstairs flushed.

A rush of resentment came, a waste of water: and then the shame as he remembered his father nagging over lights left on, "You burn enough electricity in this house to run a power station"; and the shame of the instinct to save a few pence over the light become his instinct of the water.

V

He climbed the stairs in the hope of making some amends. It was not an easy life with him in this place, and she had followed him from her own country away. He'd offered her little, he thought, the day they married; a morning waking into electric light, left on because of the bedbugs.

She had to be at rehearsals at nine. Over the coffee they hadn't talked as she went through her script. They'd arranged to meet in the bookshop beside the theatre as she left, a half-hour before the wedding. He remembered watching her stand in the sealskin cap and white lambswool coat at the bus stop until the bus came. In less than three hours they'd be married. A man is born and marries and dies, it'd be the toll of the second bell, one more to come, and there'd be no ceremonies to cover it over, no ring, no gold or silver, no friends, no common culture or tongue; they'd offered each other only themselves, but their bodies had been given before.

He'd forgot the passport as he'd left the flat and had to go back, and was already late when he left the house they'd moved to from the actors' house a second time, the house of the bedbugs and electric light at night and the stairs full of the smell of years of fish and meat stews.

It was All Souls' Day and the candles shone against the snow on the graves between the avenues of birches through the bus windows after crossing the bridge past the Alko factory, and there'd be no photos of this wedding; candles would burn in the church he'd lapsed from if they'd married there, as hands later would gently drop the old bones between the clay and their new wood before the shovels started.

Her hands were trembling on the magazine in the bookshop when he came late, "I thought you'd taken the plane."

"I am sorry. I forgot the passport."

"You didn't want to come?"

"We better hurry because we're late."

The hall was as an unemployment exchange. She'd the

same script as at breakfast, and made notes on its margins as they waited on the chairs.

"It's for the afternoon rehearsal," she'd explained.

A couple, in their early fifties, the man bald in a grey suit, and the woman in pink taffeta, heavily made-up, and with roses; they were chatting and laughing with a couple very like themselves who were their witnesses.

"What kind of people are they?" he'd asked to cover nervousness.

"Probably married so often already that the church has refused them and they have to come here," and she went on writing on the margins of the script.

When they were called she asked the two porters to act as witnesses, tipped them when they agreed, and they followed sheepishly to the doorway of the room and remained there during the ceremony, neither fully in nor out. The mayor stood with the chain of his office on his breast behind a leather-topped desk.

When the mayor asked the man to put the wedding ring on her finger they had none, and he looked on in disapproval as she took the silver ring with the green stone the sculptor who'd been killed in the car crash had given her, and the man put it on her wedding finger. It was with the same distaste the mayor called the porters from the doorway to sign the certificate, but they were married, and as he paid the fee she joked, "The divorce will cost much more."

They had coffee close to the harbour.

"It seems as if nothing has happened," they said over the cups, and she went back to rehearsals, he bought wine and meat, and returned by bus past the glimmer of candles from the graveyard to switch on all the electric lights in the flat; two-thirty on the clock and already the dusk deepening fast.

It was the night of the Arts Ball and their wedding quarrel began in the depression of bands and alcohol.

"You didn't want to marry me," she'd said.

"I was there, wasn't I?"

"You deliberately left that passport behind."

"I wouldn't have gone back for it if I did."

"You resented being married to me—it was unconscious."

"I hate that house of bugs. We need never have moved from the actors'."

"Never have moved when they asked me at the theatre every day if I had the fly-by-night sailor in their flat yet!"

It grew, until she threw the glass of whiskey stinging his eyes, and they ran from each other in the snow, big snowflakes drifting between the trees. She went to a hotel, and he back past the candles, now covered under snow, to the electric-lit room.

Was this whole day to be the shape of their lives together?

VI

The door to the roof balcony was open at the head of the stairs, and on the balcony she lay naked on the yellow bands of the collapsible deck chair, a bundle of old press cuttings by her head. She was examining an article about her in a woman's magazine, it had coloured pictures of her and had been written three years before.

"You are taking sun?"

"Why don't you come and take sun too?" she asked.

"I will later. You are reading about yourself?"

"It's by Eva who used to live with me. She wanted to put in that I always slept under the pillow. She thought that'd be of much interest to her readers. I didn't let her," she was happy and laughing.

"Do you ever want to go back to the theatre?"

"No, no. I married you to get out of the theatre. It's a system of exploitation."

"How?"

"Everybody is abused and kicked, down to the actor who is the most kicked of all. It's pure fascism."

"You'd never get anything done if someone didn't impose his will on it."

"That's what we've been taught and we must unlearn it. There should be complete participation for everybody."

"It wouldn't work."

He turned towards the sea. A woman was riding side-saddle past on the dirt-track on a mule. She was all in black against the sea, shaded by a black umbrella she held above her head with the same hand as she held the reins.

"That's nothing but capitalistic propaganda," she said; and the conversation was already boring the man.

"What would you replace them with?" he inquired concealing his irritation.

"With machines. Machines."

"And say if I don't want to go to see machines? If I want to go to see people?"

"The machines will replace them so well as to make actors obsolete."

"Do you know what I was thinking?" he changed to

I

avoid a quarrel. "The night you came from the theatre, first night of *The Dragon*, with all the roses, and we'd to search down in the roses for the one bottle of champagne."

"Do you love me as much as you did then?" she asked.

"Yes. I love you as much," and he knew less and less what love was.

"It'd be nice if we could have birches and lakes and snow and the white white houses here as well as sun and sea."

"It'd be nice, and no sharksmell," he agreed.

"And no sharksmell," she laughed.

VII

"The cabbages," she cried. "I didn't see to the cabbages. The day he was killed he wrote from the front for me to see to the cabbages."

"Why did he ask you?"

"I was the farmer one, I had the blonde hair, he wrote to me to look after the cabbages. I didn't see to the cabbages."

"Why the cabbages?" the man tried to rock her quiet in his arms, stroking the straight blonde hair.

"He was starting to grow cabbages, father did, it was his plan, he wanted to spread out the earning, so as not to have to depend for all the money on the trees."

"How was he killed?" the man realized he'd made a mistake in asking, the crying worsened, but perhaps it was better for her to cry the disturbance completely away.

"In the forest. The soldiers were nervous. He was coming back from reconnoitring the Russian lines. The men were nervous. They thought they were Russians in the forest. His Sergeant was killed too, but the two soldiers behind escaped.

"They took the coffin out from the other coffins when the lorry brought him to the farm. And I didn't see to the cabbages."

"If it wasn't the cabbages it would be something else," he said. "All lives are so fragile that when they go forever we must feel we have betrayed them in some way," he tried to say.

"I didn't see to the cabbages," she sobbed but quieter, and then, "I'm sorry to break down like this."

"It doesn't matter. It's all right. Why don't we go for a swim?"

"Let's go for a swim." She suddenly smiled. "Let's go for a swim."

Everybody got the same blows in some way or other, he thought as they changed into bathing costumes. Now in this house they were busy making miserable their passing lives, when it should be as easy to live together in some care or tenderness.

"I didn't see to the cabbages. I didn't see to the cabbages," would not leave his head.

VIII

The bus passed them in a cloud of white dust, trussed fowl and goats and rabbits hanging out of the sides, as they walked away from the house and rotting shark. All the seats in the bus were full and men were standing. On the shore oil and tar started to cling to their ropesoles.

"It'll be nice when the shark disappears and we can swim down from the house again," the woman said, she'd started to hum.

"We won't have this oil and tar," and the words seemed to hang in their ineffectiveness on the air.

They swam far out, the woman was the better swimmer, and twice she swam under the man, laughing as her yellow cap surfaced on his other side, and then they lay on their backs, and let the waves loll them, closing their eyes because of the blue fierceness of the light. They started touching each other on the thighs and breasts until the woman said, "It's so long since we had a fuck! Why don't we go in and have a fuck now?"

"Why not," he said. "We'll go in."

They got the rope-soled sandals off the rock and walked unsure now in the knowledge of what they were about to do. Beyond the house and shark the Canadian's grey Rolls was being polished for its monthly outing to the bank in Murcia.

In the play on the white sheet of the bed when the man went to part the lips of the woman's sex she pushed him away.

"Your fingers don't excite me. Your penis excites me. It's your penis I want in me. It makes me feel like being— curse it, it's another word I don't know."

She was about to reach for the dictionary when the man said, "No," and drew her to him. He tried to make up what each gallon cost of the load of water that had been put in the pool that morning to postpone his coming, but he still came long before her; and then, afraid he'd go limp, held her close for her to pump him until she came with a blind word in her own language, and as he listened to her panting it seemed that their small pleasures could hardly have happened more separately if they'd each been on opposite ends of the beach with the red house of the Canadian between.

It had not seemed as this once though there had always been trouble, and there'd been less talk of rights and positions, less talk of the fashionable psychologists in paperback on the floor by her side of the bed.

"Do you think I could go to an analyst when we get back to London?" She turned towards him from the white sheet, washed at the stone trough of the fontana by old Maria's hands. He started: it was as if she'd touched too close to his thought.

"Why do you want?"

"Our relationship would get much better."

"But how would it do you good?"

"All this summer I've got insights into myself and they'd come much quicker and clearer with an analyst."

"You get these insights reading these books?"

"Yes. Much, much insights."

"It'd cost a lot of money to go to an analyst."

"I'd be brisker and do many more translations. It'd be easier for you to work too since the relationship would be much better."

"Our relationship was good once without benefit of analysis."

"But it was built on a false foundation," she said with fierce energy, and the man turned his face away towards the sea to conceal his bitterness.

"Maybe we could both go to the analyst," she said.

If he'd to go to an analyst he'd return to the Catholic church and go to confession, which would at least be cheaper. He cursed secretly but answered, "No, I won't go but you can go to an analyst if you think it'd do good."

"Much, much good," she said, "and our lives'll be much happier. I won't spend any more times in bed depressed and crying. We'll be happy."

"We'll be happy," the man said.

Later, as he got the Vespa out of the garage, he heard the clean taps of her typewriter come from the upstairs room.

IX

He drank beer in the café on the square and watched El Cordobés fight in Madrid on the television as he waited for the correo to come up from Garrucha. When the mule passed the café with the postman and grey correo bags, he looked at the clock. It would take them more than half an hour to sort the mail.

He didn't pay for the beer but motioned to the barman that he'd be back at the end of the half-hour; it was a recognized habit by this time and the barman nodded back; if there was mail he'd come back to read it over a last beer at the café.

Ridges of rock were stripped on the road that ran uphill between low white houses to the correo. The mule was tethered to the black bars of the window and he'd to wait outside with the mule since the small room was crowded with black-shawled women. A muttering came from behind the closed grille, where the postman and drunken postmaster were sorting the mail. When the grille was drawn noisily back the postmaster stared out at the women over spectacles and shouted, "Extranjeros." The women made way for the man to go up to the grille.

"English," the postmaster shouted, reek of garlic and absinthe on his breath; he then continued as loudly in some garbled imitation of English, and started to slowly count out the letters for the foreigners of the place. As he counted each letter he shouted his imitation English but he counted slowly so that the man could read the names and take any letter addressed to him; he could have taken any letter he wished, for all the postmaster would know, but there was only one letter for him, it was from London, and a letter for his wife from her old theatre. The postmaster's performance was meant to impress the women with his knowledge of English, but they winked and laughed throughout. As the man gratefully left he heard a woman shout some bawdry at the postmaster and his threats to clear the post office.

He went back over the stripped rock and clay to the café, and waited until the beer came before opening his letter, a letter from his publisher enclosing reviews of his last book. It was never easy to read through reviews, and he read through them quickly when the beer came. It was much as listening to talk about you from another room, and the listener cares little about the quality of the talk as long as it is praise. Always the poor reviews rankled and remained, they were probably nearer the truth in the long run. To publish was to expose oneself naked in an open market, and if the praise was acceptable he could hardly complain of the ridicule, since one always had the choice to stay in original obscurity.

The editor's letter was inquiry about how the new book was coming along, in the sun of Spain it should ripen into something exciting. In the sun of Spain not a line had been written or was likely to be.

"I have known writers who failed. Who stopped writing. And they stank to themselves. And to everybody else," had been said once before to him when he'd not written for long.

"Why don't you stink then?" he'd asked.

"I have no talent. I never began."

"Couldn't I go and become a good doctor or something and probably do a great deal more good in the world?"

"Yes, but you'd rot on yourself," he remembered the argument had grown rancorous.

"I'll probably rot anyhow but it's nice you're so interested in my possible stink."

"I know them that failed. It's a worse failure than any other. They're despicable. Though if it happened it wouldn't change the friendship. That is separate."

"Why should it be worse than any other?"

"I don't know. It's more personal than any other. Perhaps the egotism is so fierce to begin with."

"It's a load of balls in my opinion."

"Besides you're too old to change."

That was perhaps true. He was too old. He paid at the counter. He would fill the red plastic container at the fontana and then go down to Garrucha and drink cognac until the fishing boats came in.

X

The man had two friends, Tomás who owned the café on the harbour, and José, an old sailor with whom he drank, buying almost all the drinks; and in return José insisted on helping him buy the fish when the boats came in. The day José's small pension came each month was the one day he bought the drinks.

The café was open but deserted, not even Tomás's son was behind the bar, so he sat outside at the red iron table and stared out on the sea that showed no sign of the returning fishing boats. He was glad to have to delay drinking, he had a too great want of cognac to sink this day out of sight.

No one passed in the white dust of the harbour, the starved greyhounds panted with lolling tongues in the shade, and he sat for half an hour until the slow flop-flop-flop of Tomás's slippers, the heels trodden down, came from the room behind the bar.

After shaking hands Tomás yawned out towards the empty sea, and then laid his head on his palm in a gesture that he'd been sleeping.

"Mucho calor," the man nodded.

"Mucho, mucho calor."

Tomás clapped his hands into the café and his son came from the back. He shouted an order and lowered his short stout body, the eyes puffed from sleep, into a chair at the table. The boy brought two cognacs, a beer and coffee on a tray.

They were on the second drink when José came, he wore a black beret and white shoes and a threadbare but neat blue suit. Cognac and coffee were brought for him by the boy and he started to talk to the man in English.

"Is the señora not well?" he asked.

"She's well but she doesn't like to come so much since that accident."

"Malo, that accident, malo," both of them nodded. Then Tomás started to speak very rapidly to José, the man could not follow all the words. One fishing boat, a black speck, had appeared far out.

"Tomás wants to know if that President Kennedy who was shot in America was a rich man?" José turned to translate after rapid speech in Spanish.

"Very rich."

"Richer than El Cordobés?"

"Much, much richer than El Cordobés."

"He had someone to leave his money to?"

"He had a large family," José translated the answers for Tomás.

There were now three boats coming home, and you could see the gulls behind the first boat. Both men nodded with satisfaction at the information that President Kennedy had a large family to leave his money to.

"Tomás says it is a very good thing that a rich man has a large family to leave his money to when he dies," José imparted.

The gulls flashed in the late sun as they dived for the guts behind the boats as they came in, and when the fish boxes were landed José bought a kilo of gambas. They'd a last drink at the bar before the man left. Once he came to the dirt-track he drove very slowly, his reactions slow and stiff from the alcohol.

XI

A candle burned between the two wine glasses, and onion and parsley were already sprinkled on the sliced tomatoes in the long yellow dish on the table. She was humming at the stove, making notes on papers scattered between the cooking utensils. She moved towards him when he came in with the white string bag of gambas, and the plastic container of water.

"I'm so happy," she said. "I was energetic. If one is energetic and works one doesn't want to stay in bed and cry."

He poured the water equally into the clay jars, jars carried on women's heads in pictures of Egypt, that stood in a wooden stand beneath the stairs.

"The table and house looks very beautiful," he said.

"One can work at the same time as cook so that one isn't just a domestic animal."

"You are doing the translations then?"

"I was afraid of it but now I feel energetic and started it after you left."

"I saw Tomás and José and got this letter for you," he was at a loss how to respond to her happiness. He would not show her his letter or the reviews, the chances were that it'd disturb her too much, he knew she had a dread that her life would be lost in his, and it would break this peace.

"They want as much translations as I can do for them. They say I am the best translator they have," she burst out of the intensity of her reading, once or twice gloating as a child in triumph.

They ate with the door closed because of the sharksmell, but they could hear the sea, and they drank white local wine with the shellfish and tomatoes and bread. She was full of plans and happy all through the meal but when they'd eaten footsteps sounded on the path to the door, a bicycle scraped against the wall. When the man opened the door it was one of the local guardia. He asked for water, and when the man offered him a chair he laid his rifle against the stairs, and sat at the table. They spoke in stumbling Spanish, the sea filling each silence and the drops of water sweating through the porous clay of the jars into the dish beneath the stand. As the guardia finished each cigarette he ground it under his boot, twisting the heel until he'd ground it into the tiles in some misguided courtesy. The last time he'd come they'd to scrape the tobacco from the tiles.

His boots were large and broken, the tops rising well above the ankles.

"Are the boots not too heavy for the heat?" the man asked after following the crushing of another cigarette butt.

"Much, much too heavy."

"Why do you wear them then?"

"It's regulations."

"Do they cost much then?"

"They cost very much." He named an exorbitant price.

"Why don't you buy a cheaper lighter pair in the shop?"

"It's not allowed. The government has given the monopoly to this man. All the guardia have to buy off the monopoly. They can charge what they like."

"It's horrible," the woman said in indignation.

"It's not fair but it is the way it is," the man answered.

"It is the way it is," the guardia said as he rose, screwing his last cigarette butt carefully into the floor and taking the gun from where it leant against the stairs. The man saw him to the door, watched his bicycle light waver into the night, before he shut the door on the sharksmell.

"This country is horrible. It is a crime to live here," the woman said fiercely as soon as he came back to the table.

"The people are not."

"They are if they accept it. As the German people were with the Nazis."

"Maybe they don't have much choice."

"You are one of them. And you give me no support. You let that man come in and ruin the evening. Don't you know that there are some people who cannot live if they have to think about the possibility of someone always being about to enter their room. I am one of these. And you give me no protection," she was sobbing fiercely as she went towards the stairs.

The man watched her go. He said or did nothing but refill his wine glass to the brim from the Soberano bottle.

XII

"Will you come with me to Garrucha?" he asked.

"There's no solutions going places," she retorted. "You buy me five postcards that you say I might like to send to my friends or you ask me to come to Garrucha and you think things are as good as they can be? Why don't you go back to yourself? Do you know that remorse originally meant going back to oneself before the word was poisoned by the popes?"

"I don't believe there are solutions."

"There are solutions if one tries hard enough. It's the same old negativism you've been drilled to accept."

"It'd be nice for me if you came to Garrucha," he wanted to avoid the argument at any cost. "I thought it'd be nice to sit at the café and watch the sea and wait for the boats to come in to buy fish."

"You want me to come with you then?"

"I do."

"That's different," she was suddenly lit with pleasure. "I don't want to go to Garrucha but I want you to want me to go to Garrucha. You'll wait for me to get ready?"

She took a half-hour to change into yellow sandals and a dress of dark blue denim that buttoned down the front and had a pocket over each breast. She asked many times as she changed if the make-up concealed the scar below the eye: but she was happy on the Vespa and sang a marching song in her own language.

José sat at the red table outside the café, and was awkward in the woman's presence until the talk came round to the Civil War.

"Yes. We shot the two priests at Garrucha. We took them out and shot them against the wall of the church. And we'd shoot them again if we got the chance," José confided with real relish.

"Good, good," the woman nodded vigorously, it was talk she loved.

"They say the communists lost the war," José's excitement brought Tomás out of the café. "The communists did not lose the war. The people of Spain lost the war. And the fascists won it."

José translated what he'd said for Tomás who nodded in his lazy way.

"Tomás is communist too but he has to be careful since he has a café," José explained.

"I'm communist as well," the woman vigorously pulled at her cigarette.

"How did you escape, José?" the man asked. "When it ended?"

"I got to Valencia, travelling at night, and got on a boat there."

"Why don't the Spanish do something, overthrow that fascist government?" the woman asked in nervous indignation. José spread his hands.

"The people of Spain are tired," he said.

A jeep came along the harbour. The magistrate and his glandular son and two farmhands were in the jeep. When the magistrate saw the woman he stopped the jeep and got out.

"You are the foreigners in Casa Smith " he introduced himself. "I've been looking for you. I've heard about you."

Tomás melted back into the café, and José went stiff on the chair.

"I know English. I like foreigners. I hate Spanish scum," the magistrate said, he was grey and lean, a glare in the eyes that sees nothing but his own obsessions.

"You will have a drink with me? Yes?" he waved and without waiting for answer he ordered three cognacs, shouting the order into the bar. Tomás's son came with the three cognacs on a tray.

"I like foreigners. I hate Spanish scum," the magistrate drank.

"These are my friends," the man said, and was about to move his cognac towards José when the old sailor's hand forbade it. José sat in petrified dignity on the chair.

"You do not know enough about Spain," the magistrate shouted. "Drink."

The man looked at José who made no movement and when the magistrate shouted again, "Drink," they both drank in bewilderment.

"We drink and now we go to see my peaches. I give you the first and finest peaches of the summer."

"I have the Vespa," the man said.

"There's plenty of place," he gestured towards the jeep.

"I have to be back for the boats."

"The jeep will take you back for the boats. Come. I give you the first and finest peaches of the summer."

XIII

A large spraying machine on metal wheels stood inside the gate of the peach orchard, and the rows of trees ran farther than the eye could follow, the loose red earth of the irrigation channels between the rows.

"Thousands of trees," the magistrate waved a manic arm and when he shouted at the two workmen they ran and turned several water taps on. Water is magic in the south of Spain and as it gushed into the channels, the red clay drinking it as fast as it ran, the magistrate's frenzy increased. The glandular son sat bored and overcome in the jeep.

"I have water for my trees," he shouted as he waved an arm towards the white moorish village that hung on the

side of the mountain, "and these scum do not have water
for their houses," he laughed in crazy triumph.

"You like my peach trees?"

"They are very fine," the man said.

"All over the world they go. To London. To Berlin. To
New York. They go from Valencia," he shouted, his eyes
hungrily on the woman's body under the blue denim dress.

"Come. I'll give you first peaches."

They followed him mesmerized to a tree of ripening
peaches, the rose blushes on the yellow in the green shelter-
ing leaves, and he drew down a branch and started to tear
free the ripe peaches. Before they could move—two, three,
four, five, six—he was ramming the peaches into the
breast pockets of the blue dress.

"I give you the first peaches of the summer," he kept
saying, and at seven, eight, when the fruit started to crush,
the juice turning the denim dark as it ran down inside the
dress, the man stepped between them.

"It's enough. I'll take any more you want," and the
magistrate's eyes reared as a mad dog at a gate and then
drew back.

"You can have plenty more peaches. Any time you
want. All summer."

"Thank you," the man said.

"I have even more water for my house than I have for
the trees," he went on, a white froth on his lips. "I have a
swimming pool full of water at my house. You come and
see my pool full of water?"

"No. We have to get back for the boats."

"But tomorrow Sunday, you come to my pool and
swim," he made the breast-stroke movement. "We can

K

swim naked in my pool. No one can see like at the sea, and after we eat peaches at a table by the pool's edge and drink white wine, wine of my grapes."

The man looked towards the woman in desperation but she stood dazed with shock or bewilderment. He didn't know how to get out of this, and he'd heard the magistrate was dangerous if crossed.

"I come at twelve then in the jeep and pick you up."

"No," the man said, desperate for time. "We'll come later on the Vespa."

"It's easier if I pick you up."

"No. I have to work first. We'll come about two on the Vespa."

"At two we'll swim and eat the peaches and drink white wine."

"Yes. We want to get back for the boats."

"I'll drive you back to the boats."

The man saw that the juice stains were wider now on the blue denim as they got into the jeep and on one side seemed stuck to her body.

At the café, where José still sat motionless as any lizard, the magistrate said as he stopped the jeep, "You soon don't see those scum any more."

"They are my friends," the man interrupted.

"It is because you don't know. Soon you know you have better friends. Tomorrow we swim and eat peaches and drink wine," he said, his eyes openly fondling the woman's body.

"At two," the man said.

XIV

José sat stiff with dignity at the red café table.

"You have been my friend, but if I see you again with that bastard: Caput," he made a chopping stroke with his hand as if breaking the back of a rabbit's neck.

"It seemed to all happen as if I had no choice."

"This time yes but not the next time."

The woman, who had remained more blank than silent, now sobbed and turned, "You see what he did, José?"

"He put the peaches in your pocket?" José looked anxiously at the man; he did not want to get in the quarrel.

When the man moved to take the peaches from the breasts she stopped him, "I am able to take them out myself."

She took them out one by one, almost all of their skins broken and the flesh crushed, and set them on the table, where three rolled to the outer rim.

"You don't want his peaches," José quietly swept the peaches from the table and they tumbled out into the dust of the roadway.

"No, no," the woman affirmed angrily. "I don't want his peaches."

She'd no longer sobbed but her face was firm against the man, who was more in despair than any shame.

The flop-flop of Tomás's slow slippers came down the café to the red tables outside.

When he'd heard the story of the orchard José translated what he'd to say, "He said he wouldn't serve that bastard. He sent his son out with the cognacs," but José added, "He has to be careful though. He has a café."

"Why is he so hated?" the man asked.

"His family were always fascists. We shot his two bro-thers, and when the fascists won he went into the Murcia jail with a bundle of birches. And he went from cell to cell till he broke every birch he had on the prisoners' backs. My brother was a prisoner there but not even a fascist pig beats shackled prisoners," José was clinched in hatred even when he broke off to translate for Tomás who nodded that it was true.

When the woman asked Tomás if she could use his back room to wash the peach juice from her dress he came with her to show her where it was, and while they were away José leaned towards the man, "If you are not careful you will lose wife. That fascist pig doesn't want to give you peaches. He wants your wife. He wants to fuck your wife."

"I know," the man said, "Will you have a drink?"

"I'll have a cognac."

The boy came with the cognacs and as the man paid he flinched at the look he thought he saw on the boy's face. The fishing boats with their flotilla of gulls flashing in the late sun were closing on the harbour. When the woman came from the back room her hair was combed so that it shone gold and her face was made-up.

"You want me to come and get some fish for you?" José asked.

"No. Not this evening," the man said, "I think we should go."

"I am ready," the woman said coldly.

As they turned away from the harbour the small figure of José got up from the table and made out of habit his way, the black beret at its usual angle, toward the incoming boats, as the greyhounds, their legs wavering under the cages of their ribs, started to come out of their porches to search for garbage in the cool.

XV

They rode in silence on the tar but when they came to the dirt-track the woman said, "Please stop." She got off the pillion seat. "I'm walking to the house. If I have to look for another husband I don't want any more scars on my face," and she looked hard and cold and tense, the profile lifted. The man drove ahead without speaking. The shark stank less in the cool, the bones wore little flesh, but he'd not be here, he thought, to see them bleach and break up in the sun: the light was good enough for him to see the flash of the lizards on the path move from a point of complete stillness to the next, out of way of the Vespa. He sat in the rocking chair with the door open waiting for her to come up the path. Her mood had not changed.

"I'd like to leave tomorrow," he said when she put down the crocheted woollen bag with the silver clasp and chain. He counted five drops of water from the clay jars drip into the bowls before she said, "Where to?" in a tense voice.

"To London. You said you wanted to go back to London."

"Running is no solution. We've been always moving. And what'll you do about your white wine and peaches?"

"We won't be here. It was why I played for two o'clock."

"Why didn't you do something when he started to push

in the peaches," she said fiercely and then the first dry sob came between the slow drips of water.

"If I hit him and wound up in a Spanish jail it'd do us all a lot of good," he said.

"You always have some excuse. You never give me any support. You know how awful it is to be married to a weak man. If I was married to a strong man like my father it would be different."

"It would be some other way but you'd be the same."

"I'd have support then. And what'll we do after London?" she stopped crying to ask, sudden demanding aggression in the voice.

"We can decide that when we get there."

"It may be decided for you this time," she threatened.

"Well then it'll be decided for me," he said.

With an explosive word he couldn't catch she climbed the stairs. He heard her turning on the bed as he got the suitcases out of the garage.

He hurriedly and raggedly got them out because of his fear of the garage, he'd been almost stung once by a scorpion nesting in an old sandal there, but when he'd the gas lamp lit and was looking about for what he'd put first in the suitcase open on the floor he heard her loudly at the cupboard as if she'd started to take out her dresses.

Later, when the man went upstairs to the room, he found she'd taken all her clothes out of the wardrobe and had arranged them on the bed ready for packing, and she was muttering, "Yes. It was no more than I deserved. I didn't see to the cabbages." Her face was hard and tense and she was not crying.

The Recruiting Officer

Two cars outside the low concrete wall of Arigna School, small and blue-slated between the coal mountains; rust of iron on the rocks of the trout stream that ran past the playground; the chant of children coming through the open windows into the rain-cleaned air: it was this lured me back into the schoolroom of this day—to watch my manager, Canon Reilly, thrash the boy Walshe; to wait for the Recruiting Officer to come—but a deeper reason than the quiet picture of the school between mountains in bringing me back, can only be finally placed on something deep in my own nature, a total paralysis of the will, and a feeling that any one thing in this life is almost as worth doing as any other.

I had got out of the Christian Brothers, I no longer wore the black clothes and white half-collar, and was no longer surrounded by the rules of the order in its monastery; but then after the first freedom I was afraid, it was that I was alone.

I had come to visit one of my married sisters, when I saw the quiet school. I said I too would live out my life in the obscurity of these small places; if I was lucky I'd find a young girl. To grow old with her among a people seemed ambition enough, there might even be children and fields and garden.

I got a school immediately, without trouble; the newly trained teachers wanted places in the university towns, not in these backwaters.

Now I am growing old in the school where I began. I have not married. I lodge in a pub in Carrick-on-Shannon, I travel in and out the seven miles on a bike to escape the pupils and their parents once the school is shut, to escape from always having to play an expected role. It is rumoured that I drink too much.

With mostly indifference I stand at the window and watch Canon Reilly shake a confession out of the boy Walshe much as a dog shakes life out of a rat; and having nothing to do but watch I think of the sea. We went to the sea in summer, a black straggle in front of Novicemaster O'Grady, in threes, less risk of buggery in threes than pairs, the boards of the bridge across to the Bull hollow under the tread of our black sandals, and below the tide washing against the timber posts. Far out on the Wall we stripped, guarding our eyes on the rocks facing south across the bay to the Pidgeon House, and when O'Grady blew the whistle we made signs of the cross on ourselves with the salt water and jumped in. He blew it again when it was time for us to get out, we towelled and dressed on the rocks, guarding our eyes, glad no sand could get between our toes, and in threes trooped home ahead of O'Grady past the wired-down idiotic palm trees along the front.

The bell for night prayers went at nine-thirty, the two rows of pews stretching to the altar, a row along each wall and the bare lino-covered space between empty of all furniture, and we knelt in the long rows in order of our rank, the higher the rank the closer to the altar. On Friday nights we knelt in the empty space between the pews and said: My very dear Brothers, I accuse myself of all the faults I have committed since my last accusation, I broke the rule of silence twice, three times I failed to guard my eyes. After a certain rank and age the guarding of the eyes wasn't mentioned, you were supposed to be past all that by then, but I never reached that stage, I got myself booted out before I became impervious to a low view of passing girls, especially on windy days.

The sea and the bell, nothing seems ever ended, it is such nonsenses I'd like written on my gravestone in the hope they'd cause confusion.

"You admit it now after you saw you wouldn't brazen your way out of it," Reilly shouts at the boy, he holds him by the arm in the empty space between the table and the long benches where the classes sit in rows, in this the schoolroom of the day.

"Now. Out with what you spent the money on."

"Lemonade," the low answer comes, the white-faced boy starting to blubber.

"Lemonade, yes, lemonade, that's how you let the cat out of the bag. The Walshes don't have shillings to squander in the shops on lemonade every day of the week."

Still gripping the boy by the arm he turns to the rows of faces in the benches.

"What sins did Walshe commit—mind I say *sins*, not one sin—but I don't know how to call it—this foul act?"

I watch the hands shoot up with more attention than I'd given to the dreary inquisition of the boy, I was under examination now.

"The sin of stealing, Canon."

"Good, but mind I said sins. It is most important in an examination of conscience before confession to know all the sins of your soul. One foul act can entail several sins."

"Lies, Canon."

"Good, but I'm looking for the most grievous sin of all."

He turned from the blank faces to look at me: why do they not know?

"Where was the poorbox when it was broken open?" I ask, having to force the question out, even after the years of inspectors I've never got used to teaching in another's presence, the humiliation and the sense of emptiness in turning oneself into a performing robot in a semblance of teaching.

"In the church, sir."

"An offence against a holy person, place or thing—what is that sin called?"

"Sacrilege," the hands at once go up.

"Good, but if you know something properly you shouldn't need all that spoonfeeding," the implied criticism of me he addresses to the children.

"Stealing, lies, and blackest of all—sacrilege," he turns again to the boy in his grip.

"If I hand you over to the police do you know where that will lead, Walshe? To the reformatory. Would you like to go to the reformatory, Walshe?"

"No, Canon."

"You have two choices then. You can either take your medicine from me here in front of the class or you can come to the barracks. Which'll you take?"

"You, Canon," he tries to appease with an appearance of total abjection and misery.

"It's going to be no picnic then. You'll have to be taught

once and for all in your life that the church of God is sacred," he raises his voice close to declamation, momentarily releases his grip on the arm, takes a length of electric wire from his pocket; the boy whimpers as quietly the priest folds it in two before taking a firm grip on the arm again.

"It's going to hurt, Walshe. But if you're ever again tempted to steal from the church you'll have something to remember!"

In a half-circle the beating moves, the boy trying to sink to the floor to escape the whistle and thud of the wire wrapping round his bare legs but held up by the arm, the boy's screaming and the heavy breathing of the priest filling the silence of the faces watching from the long benches in frightened fascination. When he finally lets go the arm the boy sinks in a heap on the floor, the moaning changing to an hysterical sobbing.

"Get up and go to your place and I hope that's the last lesson you'll have to be ever taught," he puts the length of wire back in his pocket, and takes out a blue cloth to wipe his forehead.

The boy cowers as he rises, arms automatically protecting the torn legs, moves in a beaten crawl to his place, plunges his face in rage and shame in the folds of his arms and continues hysterically sobbing.

"Open your geographies and get on with your study of the Shannon," I say as the heads turn to Walshe. There's the flap of the books being opened, they find the page, stealing a quick furtive look towards the boy as they bend their heads. In the sobbing silence the clock ticks.

"An example had to be made to nip that blaguardism in the bud," he turns to me at the window.

"I suppose."

"How do you mean *suppose*?" the eyes are dangerous.

"I suppose it was necessary to do."

"It *was* necessary," he emphasizes and after a pause, "What I'd like to see is religious instruction to counteract such influences after Second Mass every Sunday. Mr. McMurrough always took it."

"It's too far for me to come from the town to take."

"I can't see any justification for you living in the town. I can't see why you can't live in the parish. The Miss Bambricks at the post office have mentioned to me that they'd be glad to put you up."

The Miss Bambricks were two church-mad old maids who grew flowers for the altar and laundered the linen.

Old McMurrough, whom I had replaced, now lay in the Sligo madhouse reciting poetry and church doctrine, had taken catechism in the church each Sunday, while the Canon waited at the gate to bear any truant who tried to escape with the main congregation back in triumph by the ear to the class in the sidechapel.

"But I am happy where I am," I said.

"And there are many in the parish who think a public house in town is no lodgings for a person who has charge of youth."

"I conduct myself there."

"I'd sincerely hope so, but, if I may say so, it's not very co-operative."

"I am sorry but I do not want to change," I answer doggedly. With bent heads the class follows each word with furtive attention, but he changes in frustration at last, "The Christian Brother will come after lunch today."

"I'll take the other children outside while he speaks to the boys."

"They're getting it very tough to get vocations. Even tougher still to keep those they do get. They're betwixt and between, neither priests nor laymen," he volunteers but I don't want discussion.

"They may be lucky."

"The backward rural areas are their great standby. Even if they don't stay the course they'll get an education which they'd not get otherwise."

"That's how I got mine."

The hurt from my own mouth was not as great if it had come from his.

"Well it was some use then."

"Yes. It was some use."

I watch him on his way, at the door he shouts a last warning to the sniffling Walshe, "I hope that'll be one lesson your life will never forget and you can count yourself lucky that there was no police."

There'd be no repercussions from the beating except Walshe'd probably get beaten again when the news travelled home, and in a few days if asked who'd scored his legs, he'd answer that he fell in briars.

I watch the black suit shiny from car leather climb the last steps to the road gate, pausing once to inspect a crack in the concrete, and I turned to wipe the blackboard, afraid of my own hatred.

"Now I'll see what you've learned about the Shannon."

Papers rustle in the benches, there's a quick expectant buzz. Outside, the three stone walls of the playground run down to the lake, the centre wall broken by the concrete lavatory, above it the rapid sparkle of pinpoint flashes of sunlight on the wings of the blackdust swarm of flies, and on the sill in a jam jar a fistful of primroses some child has gathered from the May banks. In the stream of sunlight across the blackboard the chalkdust floats, millions of white grains, breathed in and out all day, found at night in the turnups of trousers, all the aridity of this empty trade.

"You, Murphy, tell me where the Shannon rises?"

A blank face answers in a pretence of puzzled concentration, and why should he know, his father's fields and cattle will see him through.

"Please sir."

The room is full of hands.

"Tell Murphy where the Shannon rises, Handley," a policeman's son who'll have to put his trust in his average wits.

"Shannon Pot, sir, in the Cuilceach Mountains."

"Can you tell the class now, Murphy, where it rises?"

"Shannon Pot, sir, in the Cuilceach Mountains," a look of triumph shows on his well-fed face as he haltingly repeats it.

"Where does it flow, Mary?"

"Southwards into Lough Allen close to the town of Drumshambo," the quick answer comes.

"What factory have they there?"

"Breffni Blossom jams."

"Anybody's father send apples there?"

Three hands.

"Prior? Tell about the sending of the apples."

"We pick them, sir. Put them in a heap, same as potatoes, but on the ground, we cover them with straw."

"Why do you cover them with straw?"

"Frost, sir."

A low knock comes on the door that leads to the infant classroom and my one assistant, Mrs. Maguire, appears. She is near retirement: the slack flesh fills the ample spaces of the loose black dress, but the face in contrast is curiously hard, as if all the years of wrestling with children had hardened it into intransigent assurance.

"When Mrs. Maguire says something Mrs. Maguire means what she says," the third-person reference punctuates everything she says. Now a look of anxious concern shows in the unblinking eyes.

"What happened with the Canon?"

"He thrashed Walshe for breaking into one of the poor-boxes."

I didn't want her to stay, though I too had often used the glow of fabricated concern to hurry or escape the slow minutes of the schoolday.

"Terrible. Awful," she echoes a dull safety, hers and mine.

"We'll talk about it at lunch then."

"The world, the world," she ponders as she withdraws to her own room.

I look at the clock, the crawl of the minutes, never the happiness of imagining it two o'clock and looking up and finding it half past three.

"Will you be an absorbed teacher where your work will be like a game or a clockwatcher?" Jordan, the Education Lecturer, had asked after a lecture, it was his custom after a lecture to select one student to walk with him through the corridor with its shine of wax and the white marble busts of the saints and philosophers on their pedestals along the walls.

"I hope I'll be absorbed, sir."

"I hope so too for your sake. I can imagine few worse hells than a teacher who is a clockwatcher, driven to distraction by the children, while the day hangs about him like lead."

I could answer him now, I was a clockwatcher, and the day mostly hung like lead, each morning a dislocation of your life in order to entice or bend their opposing wills to yours, and the day a concentration on this hollow grapple, but it seems good as anything else and it's easier to stay than move.

"We'll leave the apples for a time and go on with the Shannon."

The class drags on until the iron gate on the road sounds. A woman comes down the concrete steps.

A mother come to complain, I think and instinctively start to marshal the reassuring clichés, "The child is sensitive, and when it loses the sensitivity will surprise us all, to force it now can only cause damage, you have nothing to worry about."

"That was my trouble so at that age, I was too sensitive, I was never understood," she'd reply.

"Thank you for coming to see me."

"I feel less worried now."

In the beginning, everybody was sensitive, and never understood, but hides hardened.

This time, no mother, a Miss Martin: she lived with her brother across the empty waste of wheat-coloured sedge and stunted birch of the Gloria bog. She made toys from used matchsticks in the winter nights.

"I wonder if I could take young Horan from his lessons for a few minutes, sir. It's the ringworm."

"Luke, see Miss Martin in the porch." The boy goes quietly out to the porch, already charmingly stolid in the acceptance of his power, Luke, magical fifth in a line of male children unbroken by girls; and while he wailed under the water of his baptism at the stone font in Cootehall church a worm was placed in his hand, either the priest didn't see or was content to ignore it, but the Horans rejoiced, their fifth infant boy would grow up with the power of healing ringworm.

On Tuesdays and on Fridays, days of the sorrowful mysteries, he touched the sores thrice in the name of the Father and Son and Holy Ghost, and the invisible worm widening the raw coin on the skin dies, power of magic and religion killing the slow worm patiently circling.

"Did you wash your hands, Luke?"

"Yes, sir. I used the soap."

"Show them to me."

"All right. You can get on with your work."

The last to come before lunch was the tinker, with pony and cart, the brass shining on the harness, to clean out the lavatory, and as I give him the key we make polite professional remarks about the flies and heat.

"Ah, but not to worry, sir, I'll bury it deep," he touches his cap. Soon, soon, they'll come and flush him and me into the twentieth century whatever the good that will do, and I grow ashamed of the violence of the thought, and as if to atone, over lunch, give Mrs. Maguire a quiet account of the poorbox.

After lunch he comes, dressed all in black, with a black

L

briefcase, the half-collar of the Christian Brother on the throat instead of the priest's full collar, a big white-haired man, who seemed made more to follow ploughing horses than to stand in classrooms. The large hand lifts the brief-case on the table.

"My name is Brother Mahon and Canon Reilly kindly gave me permission to speak to the senior boys about a vocation to the Irish Christian Brothers." I wonder if he knows I too had been once as he is now; if he looks at me as a rotten apple in the barrel, but if he does he says nothing, all glory to the power of the Lie or Silence that makes people easy in the void, all on our arses except the helping hand they give us on our way.

"I told Canon Reilly I'd take the other children out to the playground while you spoke."

"Lucky to have such a fine manager as the Canon, takes a great interest in schools."

"Couldn't ask for a better manager," I answer, the brick supports the brick above it, I'm a rogue and you're another. "I'll just take them outside now."

"All except the boys of the sixth class take your English book and follow me outside," and again, because I feel watched, the voice is not my own, a ventriloquist's dummy that might at any minute fall apart.

The Brother motions the scattered boys closer to the table, "It'll only be just a man to man chat," as I take the others out, to sit against the white wall of the school in the sun, facing the lake, where the tinker is putting the green sods back above the buried shit, the flies thick above the cart and grazing pony.

Through the open window the low voice drifts out into

the silence of the children against the wall in the sun, and I smile as I listen, if one could wait long enough everything was repeated. I wonder who'll rise to the gleaming spoon and find the sharpened hooks as I did once.

"I want you to imagine a very different lake shore to your own little lake below your school.

"Hot sands," his words drift out. "Palm trees, glittering sea, tired after fishing all the night and washing their nets, tall dark man comes through the palms down to the water.

"We have laboured all the night and have taken nothing, the fishermen answer. The two boats were so full of fish that they began to sink, after they put out at his word, fall on their knees on the sand, and the tall man for it was Jesus lifted them up and said to them follow me, from henceforth you will catch men.

"In this schoolroom two thousand years later I bring you the same message. Follow me and catch men. Follow me into the Irish Christian Brothers, where as teachers you will lead the little children He so loved to Christ.

"For death comes as a thief in the night, the longest life is but a day, and when you go before the Judgement Seat can you without trembling say to Jesus I refused the call even the tired fishermen answered, and what if He refuses you as you refused Him."

He sends them out into the porch, and brings them back one by one to interview them alone, while the tinker hands me back the keys, "I've buried it deep, sir. There'll be no flies," and the rise and fall of voices comes from Mrs. Maguire's infant prison house *Eena, meena, mina moo, capall, asal agus bo.*

Name, age, your father's farm? he asks and more to silence my own memory than the low chatter of the children I force, "Come on now, get on with your reading," but after they grow silent to covertly read my real mood the chatter grows loud again.

"You have listened to all that I've said?" I'd been asked once too.

"Yes, Brother," I'd answered.

"Do you think you could spend your life as a Christian Brother?"

"I'm not sure, Brother."

"Do you think your parents would have any objection?"

"I don't know, Brother."

"What do you say we go and have a little talk with them after I've seen the rest of the boys?"

It was finished then, my mother's face had lighted when he drove me home, "It'd be an honour to have a Christian Brother in the family." "He'll get a free education too, the best there is," and that August I was in the train with the single ticket, fear of the unknown rooms and people. My brother inherited the bare acres in my place, and married, and with the same strength as she had driven me away he put her in a back room with the old furniture of her marriage while his new wife reigned amid the new furniture of the best rooms; and now each summer I take her to her usual small hotel at the sea, and I walk by her side on the sand saying, "Yes and yes and yes," to her complaints about my brother and his wife until she tires herself into relief and changes "Do you think should I go to the baths after lunch?" "Go to the baths, it'll do your arthritis good."

"I think I'll go then."

I want to ask her why she wanted the acres for my brother, why she pushed me away, but I don't ask, I walk by her side on the sand, and echo her life with "Yes and yes and yes," for it is all a wheel.

A light tap comes on the classroom window, a gesture of spread hands that he is finished, and I take the children in. Two of the boys have been set apart, with their schoolbags.

"I'm driving John and Jim to their houses, we'll talk over everything with their parents."

"I hope it'll be all right."

"We'll see that everything is made clear. Thank you for your help."

After the shaking of hands I turn to the board but I do not want to teach.

"Open your English books and copy page forty-one in your best handwriting."

I stand at the window while the nibs scrape. Certainly nothing I've ever done resembles so closely the shape of my life as my leaving of the Holy Brothers; having neither the resolution to stay on or the courage to leave, the year before Final Vows I took to bed and refused to get up.

"The doctor says you're in perfect health. That there's nothing the matter with you," old Cogger, the boss, had tried to reason. "So why can't you get up when we are even shortstaffed in the school?"

"I can't get up."

"What's wrong with you that you can't get up?"

"Nothing."

"If you don't get up I have no option but to report you to General Headquarters."

I did not get up, he had no option, and the result was an

order for my dismissal, but as quietly as possible so as not to scandalize my brothers in J. C. or the good people of the town. Old Cogger showed me the letter. I was to get a suit of clothes, underwear, railway ticket and one pound. It revived me immediately. I told him the underwear I had would do and he raised the one pound to five.

The next hurdle was how to get my fit in clothes in a small town without causing scandal. Old Cogger dithered till the day before I had to leave, but at nightfall brought home two likely fits. I picked one, and packed it, and off we set by bus for Limerick, to all appearances a young Christian Brother and an old on some ordinary business to town, but old Cogger would come back alone. We did not speak on the way.

Behind a locked door and drawn curtains I changed in the guest room of the house in Limerick. I've wondered what happened to the black uniform I left behind, whether they gave it to another C.B. or burned it as they burn the clothes of the dead. Cogger showed me to the door as I left for the train but I can't remember if he wished me luck or shook hands or just shut the door on my back. I had a hat too, yes a brown hat and a blue suit, but I didn't realize how bloody awful they looked until I met my sisters on O'Connell Bridge. They coloured with shame, afraid to be seen walking with me they rushed me into a taxi and didn't speak until they had me safely inside the front door of the flat, when one doubled up on the sofa unable to stop laughing, and the other swore at me, "In the name of Jasus what possessed the Christians to sail you out into the world in a getup the like of that or you to appear in it." Though what I remember most was the shock of *sir* when the waiter said

"Thank you, sir," as I paid him for the cup of tea I had on the train.

Even if the memories are bitter they still quicken the passing of time. It is the sly coughing of the children that tell me the hands have passed three.

"All right. Put your books away and stand up."

In a fury the books are put away and they are waiting for me on their feet.

"Bless yourselves."

They bless themselves and chant their gratitude for the day.

"Don't rush the door, it's just as quick to go quietly."

I hear their hoops of joy go down the road, and I linger over the locking up. I am always happy at this hour, it's as if the chains of the day were worth wearing to feel them drop away. I feel born again as I start to pedal towards the town. How, how, though, can a man be born again when he is old? Can he enter a second time his mother's bag of tricks? I laugh at last.

Was it not said by *Water* and the *Holy Spirit*?

Several infusions of whiskey at the Bridge Bar, contemplation of the Shannon through its windows: it rises in the Shannon Pot, it flows to the sea, there are stranger pike along its banks than in its waters, will keep this breath alive until the morning's dislocation.